—— A BIT OF ——

Irish Gold

Enjoy

this Irish Journey

Phyllis Karenia

A BIT OF

Irish Gold

A LOVE STORY

By

PHYLLIS KARSNIA

iUniverse, Inc.
Bloomington

A Bit of Irish Gold
A Love Story

iUniverse books may be ordered through booksellers or by contacting:

iUniverse
1663 Liberty Drive
Bloomington, IN 47403
www.iuniverse.com
1-800-Authors (1-800-288-4677)

ISBN: 978-1-4759-6996-2 (sc)
ISBN: 978-1-4759-6998-6 (hc)
ISBN: 978-1-4759-6997-9 (ebk)

Library of Congress Control Number: 2013900466

Printed in the United States of America

iUniverse rev. date: 01/14/2013

Table of Contents

SECTION I IRISH IMMIGRANT

SECTION II IRISH CORRESPONDENCE

SECTION III   IRISH PIONEERS

Section I

Irish Immigrant

Chapter 1

STARTING A JOURNEY
1888

"VISAS." The word exploded through the window. Matt stopped abruptly, hesitating for only a second before pushing open the door. He'd dreamed of going to America for many years and maybe that tattered sign in the window was a wee bit of luck. He swallowed hard for courage but his voice squeaked when he blurted out, "I'd like a visa for America."

Busy writing, the clerk didn't look up. "Quota's filled."

"Quota?" The word sounded threatening.

"No more visas. Immigration's closed. Irish have been fleeing Ireland like flies and the immigration quota's filled."

Closed. Filled. Eight years of yearning . . . My dream destroyed . . . Matt's legs felt as wobbly as a newborn colt's and he grabbed the counter for support. *I've waited too long!* Glancing up, the clerk saw Matt's dazed look. A wave of compassion compelled him to put down his pencil. Leaning back in his chair he said, "Visas are still available in Scotland. Go to Glasgow—ships sail to America from Glasgow."

The workhorses plodded home without guidance from Matt. The reins hung loosely in his hands as he slouched on the wagon seat, frowning in thought. Matt had been surprised that morning when Kelly, the manager of the O'Brian estate, told Matt to go to town for supplies all alone. Matt had never gone without Da.' *I wonder if Kelly suspects Da' spends his time in the pub while I do the work.* After he loaded supplies on the wagon, Matt couldn't resist enjoying a bit of freedom before returning to the estate. *This is my first opportunity to explore the town. Sure, and 'twas luck took me to that sign in the window. Such a small town, but I've never walked in front of that store before. That's what little freedom I have.*

Anger bubbled up as he thought about what little control he had of his life. *I cannot steal a horse. Kelly would catch me and string me up alive. Should I wait for the quota to be reopened? But when would that be?* Between clenched teeth he vowed to himself, *I'll not let go of my dream. 'Tis to Glasgow I'll go. I'll go to Belfast and take the ferry across the Irish Sea to Scotland.* The horses twitched their ears as he stood on the wagon and shouted to them: "I can do it! I'm going to America!" Matt's brow was still creased from concentration as he settled his team in their stalls.

In the morning while currying the horses, Matt told his brother Timmy what he'd found out. "'Tis time for me to go. I'm eighteen."

Matt's older brother Patrick left the day their Da' up and married sixteen-year-old Betty Walsh four months after his wife, Marie, died in childbirth. Betty, the daughter of a shoveler in the barns, had been hired to care for newborn Timmy. Shovelers received fewer wages than horse handlers; the Walsh family lived in squalor amidst the cluster of hovels huddled outside the imposing stone fence enclosing the estate. Betty, appreciative of improving her pitiful existence, cared for Timmy tenderly.

Patrick and Matt had been devastated at their mother's death, but when Da' began drinking afterward, their pain at losing her was compounded. Matt still longed for the tiny woman who had brought so much cheer into their lives. As one of the cooks at the mansion, she fed them tidbits of gossip and leftover food. She soothed her husband during his black Irish moods and outbursts of temper.

When Da' and Betty drunkenly announced their marriage and Patrick took off, ten-year-old Matt felt an ache deep in his heart. To console himself, Matt vowed to leave as soon as he turned fifteen.

Meanwhile, Betty's interest in Timmy decreased as her pregnancy progressed, and Matt became Timmy's surrogate mother.

Five years later, Timmy's position was replaced by two younger brothers, Terry and Michael. Young Betty not only neglected Timmy, but her own babies. Matt did what he could for all the wee ones. Furious with Da' for drinking up his meager wages but worried about the family's welfare, Matt postponed his dream.

Ironically, it was Thomas who triggered Matt's hasty departure. A few days following Matt's trip to Donaghmore, Thomas came home from the pub drunker and meaner than usual. His sons all cowered out of his way, but he still managed to smack each one. When he turned on Betty, Matt rushed in and shoved his Da' down on the bed. Standing with clenched fists, Matt watched as his father struggled a few seconds before falling back into a drunken slumber.

Matt stood motionless, grieving at how his mother's death had changed their lives, and then fled to his cot in the corner of the room. Gathering up the few clothes he owned, he ran out the door and into the woodshed to dig up the scant savings he had buried. At the last minute he snatched up an old horse blanket tossed in a corner.

From out of the darkness, he heard Timmy's soft whisper: "'Bye, Matt!"

Matt turned to his younger brother, who had followed him out. Timmy held out a loaf of oat bread. "I grabbed this off the table, Matt. You'll need food."

Matt hugged the boy. "I hate to leave you, Timmy, but I have to get away before I kill our Da'"

Timmy held on to Matt, squeezing hard, his wet face buried into his older brother's chest. Matt choked on his own tears. Knowing this day had been coming, Timmy managed to whisper, "Good luck, Matt. I'll miss you."

Matt ruffled the boy's hair, kissed him on the forehead, then turned and quickly left before he changed his mind.

Timmy had been Matt's shadow since he could toddle, following Matt around as he took care of the horses and sheep on the prosperous estate. As he worked, Matt would grumble to Timmy about conditions in Ireland. "Since 1690 Catholics in Ireland have suffered from British occupation. Now it's 1888 and Protestant landowners still live in castles while the Irish die in poverty." Matt had given up hope that Irish rights would ever be restored. Every year his family became poorer. "I've heard that in America, anybody can own land. America. That's where I'll be going. 'Twill never happen here, not at all."

Although he didn't grasp everything Matt was saying, Timmy had understood that he intended to leave Ireland. When Matt's raging stopped, Timmy would plead, "Don't go yet, Matt. Please." And Matt would soften, temporarily setting aside thought of America.

But this was it! Matt, teeth clenched in fury, hardened his heart and hurled himself away from his brother. As he walked past the estate, the outline of the castle owned by the O'Brian family loomed in the distance, barely visible in the fading evening light. The crude cottage where Matt and his family lived was placed behind the barns so the thatched roof couldn't be seen from the mansion. The sight would have ruined the pastoral scene viewed from the windows of the castle. A river, swirling its way from the Irish Sea, zigzagged across the emerald green lawns like a snake.

Sheep kept the grass eaten down so the fields were a perfect length of green for the polo field. Polo was a passion of the O'Brians and their friends. The players whacked at balls from the back of the horses, but mistreated the animals after their game was ended. Matt began sharing his Da's responsibility for the horses at an early age. These days, Da' spent most of his day in the pub while Matt cared for the horses as though they belonged to him. He found it increasingly difficult to hold his temper when he saw the horses treated badly.

Walking down the dark path in front of the castle, Matt vowed out loud, "You'll see. Someday I'll own land in America." At the edge of the property he turned for a last look. Shaking his fist, he spat, "I'll never be back!"

As familiar territory disappeared, Matt experienced mixed feelings. One minute he was jubilant because he was finally leaving, the next gripped with fear of the unknown. Worry about his brothers was a heavy black cloud of guilt that almost made him turn back.

Propelled on by his dream, Matt told himself, *'Tis glad I am the fight with Da' forced me into going.*

His courage declined as the distance widened between him and the estate. He'd never been past Donaghmore and, unsure of the way, his steps slowed. To keep from turning back, he recited his reasons for leaving: *I've been helping Da' since I was a wee lad. Now, I do the work of two men while Da' sneaks off to the pub and then staggers home meaner every day, yelling and cuffing at all of us. Maybe he'll stop drinking without me there. He won't change while I'm doing his job. Conditions in Ireland will never change, either. Would I ever own a scrap of land? Do I want to slave for bloody O'Brians the rest of my life?*

Convinced that life in America would be better, Matt walked faster.

Chapter 2

PRAYERS IN ARMAGH
1888

The moon lit Matt's way for hours before he fell down exhausted in a grove of trees. Wrapped in the horse blanket and using his knapsack for a pillow, he allowed himself only a few hours of sleep before setting out again at dawn. Matt checked his directions with the rising sun, fearful of not heading north. He walked past miles of rolling green pastures with grazing livestock inside stone fences. An occasional farmer waved in the distance, temporarily relieving feelings of terrible loneliness.

At dusk Matt hid in the woods close to a small cottage. Shivering in the damp night air as he waited for the lantern light to be snuffed out, he was glad winter was over, although May weather still could be fickle with its bone-chilling dampness. The cottage finally went dark.

Not sure of what animals he'd find inside the barn, he carefully pushed open the door of the small stone structure huddled next to the cottage. Two cows turned their heads to stare at him. Hoping the cows wouldn't moo and wake the farmer, he stood quietly until they turned away indifferently. The familiar smells of hay and manure comforted him as he hunkered down with his horse blanket on stacks of hay. Scratching absent-mindedly, he thought, *I'm glad I rescued this old horse blanket when Kelly threw it away.* Physically and emotionally exhausted, he was instantly sound asleep.

When the cows began stirring before daylight, Matt jumped up, anxious to leave before the farmer found him. "First, I'll have a wee bit of that milk," he said to one of the cows. Snatching his cap off, he directed the stream of milk into its brim. Although the cow swished her tail, she allowed Matt to milk her and he patted her flank to thank her. But he couldn't waste time and, feeling revived from the warm nourishing milk, Matt set off at a good pace.

Trudging steadily, Matt covered many miles. By mid-morning the drizzle had turned into a heavy rain. Besides getting soaked, he was becoming confused about directions. Crossing over a long rolling hill, he suddenly saw a flock of sheep with a man herding them from behind. Matt shouted, "Hello! Hello!"

The farmer turned around with a startled look on his face. Then he gave him a wave and stood waiting. Panting from running, Matt said, "'Tis glad I am to see you. I'm on my way to Belfast. Can you tell me if I'm going north?"

"Sure, and you are. 'Twas a start you gave me, appearing out of nowhere. Thought I was seeing a ghost. Not many people walk these hills. Where did you come from? But I'm forgetting my manners. My name is Sean Cullen."

"Matt Donahue. I came from Donaghmore, County Louth. This is my third day of walking and I've not talked to another soul. You're the first person I've seen today."

While they talked, Sean ushered his sheep through a gate in a short stone fence. He slammed the gate shut and looked at Matt again. "You look cold and wet. It's a hot cup of tea you need. My wife, Clare, will be happy for the company. C'mon."

Sean's plump wife was as cheerful as the painted red door of their cottage. She made Matt sit in front of the fireplace to warm up while the water boiled in the kettle. Taking scones out of the oven, she put them on a plate and beckoned him over to the table. The tantalizing smell had his stomach growling. "Thanks, Mrs. Cullen," Matt said as she poured hot steaming tea for him.

"Call me Clare," she said as she sank into another chair.

"And you're off to Belfast?" Sean asked as they waited for the tea to cool.

"I'm going to Belfast to catch the ferry to Scotland. I'm sailing to America."

They exclaimed over the great adventure Matt had ahead of him. Sean asked, "Do you have family there?"

"No. Nobody. I've wanted to go for a long time." Matt paused before adding, "I want to own my own land."

"Aren't you the brave lad! Most people have somebody sending for them and waiting for them when they arrive." The friendly farmer insisted on giving him a ride to Monaghan. He looked out at the rain running down the window. "'Tis a soft day, a good day to go to town for supplies. Clare has a long list for me."

Sean went outside to hitch up the wagon. As Clare poured more tea for Matt she said, "Sure, and 'tis no trouble for Sean to take you, not at all. Won't he be enjoying a pint of Guinness at his favorite pub?" The hot tea warmed Matt's belly, but the Cullens' hospitality warmed his heart.

The ride gave his aching body a rest after walking over hills all day. Sean told him, "This is the Cooley Peninsula area, a good pastureland for the sheep. I've lived here all my life; I was born here, and my father before me." As the sun peeked out Matt admired the lush rolling green hills glistening with raindrops.

Sean questioned Matt more about what his plans were when he arrived in America. "My own brother sailed away two years ago, but we've not heard from the buggar at all, not at all. When he left, he promised to send money for us to join him."

"I have no plans yet. First I have to get work on a freight ship to pay for my passage."

"What does your poor mother think about your leaving?"

"My mother died when I was ten. When Da' remarried, my older brother left home. He's disappeared these eight years without a word. I promised myself I'd leave when I was fifteen just like he did. Da' started drinking and I stayed to help with the babies that started coming. I took care of the horses on the O'Brian estate, doing my Da's work and mine too. 'Tis past time I leave."

"They say America is a wonderful place. Filled with opportunities. I think you'll do well."

Matt asked, "How far is it to Dungannon? I have an aunt in Dungannon but I don't know her name because she's married since she left Donaghmore. 'Twould be good to see her before I leave."

"Dungannon is about a day's walk, but 'twill take you out of your way for Belfast. You would go through Armagh and then to Dungannon. But toward the sea is a faster route for Belfast."

In the center of Monaghan, Sean dropped Matt off at a large drinking fountain with an ornate canopy supported by marble columns. "Good-bye and good luck to you, lad. I hope you find your land at journey's end."

"Thanks to you and your wife for being so generous to me." Matt waved good-bye as the horses clip clopped over the cobble-stoned street.

While taking a long drink of water from the fountain, Matt made up his mind to ignore the shorter route to Belfast. *With Armagh only an afternoon's walk away, how can I leave Ireland without paying my respects to St. Patrick, the Patron Saint of Ireland? Can I leave Ireland without saying good-bye to my kind Aunt Kate? Sure, and St. Patrick himself and my aunt would both put the curse on me.*

The food and rest spurred Matt on for a few more hours. At dusk he entered the town of Armagh. Wandering the streets in awe, he told himself, *I can't believe I'm in the most famous city in Ireland. Sure, and 'twas the year 432 when St. Patrick sailed to Armagh.* Matt remembered his history lessons from Father Finnerty very well. He hadn't been allowed to go back to school after his mother died, but like most Irishmen he loved learning. Marie wanted her sons educated, but after Patrick left, his father expected Matt to replace his brother in the barn and his mother at home. His schooling was over.

St. Patrick's Cathedral guarded the town from a high hill. Looking up at it, he crossed himself. *The cathedral honoring the Patron of Ireland will keep me safe,* Matt assured himself as he ran up the steep path.

Parishioners streamed out of the huge church. Matt hid in the shadows until it was safe to slip through the door unnoticed. Father

Finnerty had visited the cathedral and told Matt about a room with hats of Cardinals dangling from the ceiling. Matt remembered him saying, "When a Cardinal's soul goes to heaven, his hat falls down." *Sure, and I'll be safer yet in a room filled with Cardinals' hats and souls.*

Matt tiptoed down the side aisle until he found the small room with dangling hats. The room smelled musty but a padded bench under the hats provided him with a bed. Lying there, Matt thought about Father Finnerty, a squarely-built man who seemed to know everything. Before Father Finnerty arrived, the tenants' children had been taught in ditches and hedges by outlaw priests and other itinerants traveling through small hamlets. Education had been erratic, lasting only as long as the travelers stayed, whether for a few days or a few weeks.

In Northern Ireland, Catholicism was not allowed and priests were always in hiding from the British. Father Finnerty had been an outlaw priest, barely escaping when the soldiers appeared while he was saying Mass in a private home in Belfast. Stopping for a rest in Donaghmore, he'd taken a liking for the place and stayed to make himself responsible for the children's schooling as well as their souls. He wore a long black beard that disappeared into his black robe. His ferocious black looks could kill boys who did not know their lessons. Matt, who learned his lessons well, became a favorite of Father Finnerty's, receiving special attention for his eagerness to learn. The days that Matt served as altar boy were enhanced by his friendship with the priest.

What would Ma think of my sleeping in a church? 'Tis worth the extra walk to come here to pay my respects to St. Patrick before leaving Ireland. His mother had taught him as much as she knew about the Catholic faith and made him learn his prayers. Saying his prayers made him feel closer to her and he faithfully recited them every night. He fell asleep praying.

Chapter 3

ANNIE IN DUNGANNON
1888

Chants from a mass awakened him. Knowing the Latin prayers, he prayed along with the chanting as he finished off the crumbs of oat bread Timmy had stolen for him. He'd rationed it carefully, breaking off small chunks to nibble. Now his food was completely gone.

About noon, hunger pangs were slowing him down and he breathed a sigh of relief when he came to a town. *Sure, and I hate parting with my money but I need to eat.* Walking around the small town square, he went into a pub where a few men sat on stools at the bar. He ordered a bowl of potato soup.

As he set the piping hot bowl in front of Matt, the bartender asked, "Where you from?"

"Donaghmore, County Louth. Is this Dungannon?" The steam from the soup wafting up to his nostrils smelled so delicious, Matt could wait no longer for a spoonful. It was so hot he could barely swallow it.

"'Tis. Dungannon, County Tyrone. You've come a long way."

"I have an aunt here—Kate Donahue she was but I don't know her married name."

The bartender shook his head. "I know of no Kate Donahue."

"The last I heard, she worked in a spool factory that makes linen thread."

"Oh, sure, and you can go to the factory and inquire about your Aunt Kate. 'Tis easy to find. Dungannon is famous for its linens."

"What about directions to Belfast? I'm on my way to Belfast and then to Scotland. I was told that I could sail to America from Glasgow."

A man watching the bubbles rising in his fresh pint of Guinness said, "Belfast 'tis thirty miles away."

A lad about his own age interrupted, "My own brother sailed away to America a few months ago. Sure, and he'll be sending for me as soon as he can save enough money."

An old man slumped over a pint turned a seamed face to Matt. "I made the trip a few times myself when I worked on the ships. 'Tis a hard journey, not to mention the fierce winds that blow up terrible storms."

Matt's stomach plunged, but he said, "I'm used to hard work. I've taken care of horses on the O'Brian estate since I was a wee lad. Do you think I can get work on a freight ship to pay for my passage?"

"You should, lad. You should," the old sailor said.

Matt whistled as he set off at a good pace when he left the pub, where he'd been filled with hope as well as with food. He'd listened to stories about America and received directions on how to get to Belfast. At Belfast he could get on a ferry crossing the Irish Sea to Glasgow.

Oranges in the window of a produce shop at the end of the block caught his attention. His mouth watered. Oranges had been a special treat at Christmas until his mother died, but he remembered the sweet juicy taste. Impulsively, he turned back to push open the door of the shop.

A brown-haired girl sitting behind the counter was concentrating on threading a needle. Matt stopped inside the doorway. "Hello."

The girl jumped. A spool of thread fell off her lap, rolling on the floor toward Matt. Matt went scrambling for the thread. He grabbed at the spool, bumping heads with the girl as she reached for it. They both straightened up holding their heads, and as they stood face to face Matt was entranced by her lively blue eyes. His pulse raced as he held out the spool, but when he noticed blood on her thumb he exclaimed, "Sure, and you're hurt!"

The girl looked down at her thumb. "'Tis nothing. I must have pricked my finger." She licked off the blood and wiped her thumb on her apron.

Matt realized he was staring at her when a blush spread across her cheeks. He felt his own face flush and stammered, "Could I—could I buy an orange?" While he dug in his pocket for change, he shyly told her, "I'm heading for Scotland to get passage on a boat to America."

Her eyes widened with admiration. "I dream about going to America," she said. "I'm Annie Rice."

"My name's Matt Donahue. I'm going to America because I want to own land and have the right to vote." Realizing suddenly that he'd blurted out too much in Protestant territory, Matt's body went rigid.

He relaxed when she warned, "Be careful going through Belfast. Mostly Protestants live there and 'tis full of English soldiers. I'll be thinking of you, Matt. Could you—would you write and let me know how you do? I'd really like that." She blushed again. "Sure, and I'll be worrying about you, wondering if you made it."

Matt gaped at this strange girl showing concern for him. Finally he stammered, "Sure, and I will. Soon as I get to New York." Just saying New York out loud gave him confidence.

"Address it to Annie Rice, Rice Produce Shop, Dungannon, County Tyrone."

Forcing himself to walk to the door, Matt placed his hand on the doorknob. Annie rushed over to the window and shoved oranges into a cloth bag. "Here, take these oranges. They'll be good for you on that long ocean voyage." Her tone turned bitter. "You need them worse than my brothers, who will gobble them up after gambling their money away."

Matt reached for the oranges, but jerked with surprise when the girl impetuously kissed him on the cheek. "The luck of the Irish be with you, Matt Donahue. God bless you and keep you safe."

Matt wandered down the street in a trance. He'd never received that much affection from anybody since his mother died. That was a long time ago. He forgot about looking for Aunt Kate until he happened upon the spool factory. The bartender had told him it was on his way out of town. The large brown factory looked forbidding and he hesitated about knocking on the thick wood door. He scolded himself, *Now that I'm here I cannot just pass on by.*

Matt knocked hard and waited. Nobody answered. Waiting for a long time after knocking hard again, Matt was about to turn away when a man opened the door. He looked angry at the interruption. "What do you want?"

"Excuse me, sir. I'm on my way to America and wanted to say good-bye to my Aunt Kate Donahue. I don't know her married name, but I know that she worked here for a long time."

"I know of no Kate Donahue. Be off with you." The door slammed.

Chapter 4

SAILING TO AMERICA
1888

Matt felt crushed. Shoulders slumped, he slowly turned away from the door. Raging under his breath at the big brute of a man who had turned him away, fond memories of Aunt Kate playing with him when he was a toddler flickered through his mind. Now he realized that his father's sister had been young herself, maybe only sixteen when she left Donaghmore to go to Dungannon. *Should I stay and search for her or go on? Sure, and she did not come back to Donaghmore to check on how I was doing after Ma died, now did she?* Ignoring the emptiness at not finding Aunt Kate, pretending he did not care that he did not find her for a family farewell, his pace quickened.

His thoughts turned to Annie. *Annie's kiss felt like a butterfly fluttering on my cheek. She asked me to write.* He looked at the bag of oranges and put his hand lightly to the spot where she'd kissed him. As he walked toward Belfast, he felt his enthusiasm about leaving diminishing, but forced himself to go on.

In Belfast, remembering Annie's warning about Protestants and English soldiers, he avoided talking to anybody. He found the ferry landing without difficulty, breathing silent thanks to the men in the pub for their explicit directions.

Standing at the railing as the ferry crossed the Irish Sea to Scotland, he looked back as Ireland faded away in the mist. Unexpectedly, he felt stunned by the feeling of utter homesickness that engulfed him. He recalled how Timmy had tearfully hugged him when they said goodbye and how often he'd protected his stepmother and half brothers. What would happen to them?

Thoughts about Annie surfaced and, stroking his cheek, he relived her kiss. *Maybe I should sail right back to Belfast on this ferry. I could find work there and go visit Annie in Dungannon.* His throat closed over and tears slid down his cheeks. It was drizzling and he lifted his face so the tears mingled with the rain. Inside the ferry it was dry and warm but Matt couldn't bear to tear himself away from the railing. This might be his last glimpse of Ireland.

When the Irish shore was no longer visible he told himself firmly: *You've great adventures ahead of you, Matt Donahue.* His fears scattered like dark clouds in the sunshine when he stepped off the ferry in Glasgow. The first part of his journey was successful! He was on his way to America! He'd write to Annie from America. Maybe she'd come to see him. That thought gave him a new dream. *Annie in America!*

Glasgow harbor was filled with ships. Matt wandered along the waterfront admiring the ships and praying for help in finding a ship sailing to America. Inside a crowded pub, he thirstily drank a glass of ale the bartender slapped on the bar. A group of men were gathered around a big man wearing a uniform. "What's going on over there?" Matt inquired.

"Captain McDougall signing up his crew. They sail for America tonight," the bartender replied.

Matt pushed off his stool and stood in front of the captain. "You're signing up crew to sail to America?" Matt was so excited he could barely get the words out.

Captain McDougall peered at him through the smoke. "Are you a sailor?"

"No, but I've worked hard all my life." Matt quivered with energy and had a steely glint of determination in his eyes.

The captain said, "Sign your name here on this paper."

Matt didn't succeed in suppressing a grin as he signed the contract.

"We'll be leaving in an hour. Climb on board now, get yourself a bunk, and get started working. Take this paper with you to show that you're hired."

Looking up at the ship, Matt was seized with a strange feeling of dread. His legs trembled and he had to use the rope to help pull himself up the gangplank. On deck, it was a bevy of activity and the officer in charge told him to stow his bundle down below on a bunk and get back up to work. When the freight ship cast off, Matt was too busy working with another sailor to notice the land slipping away.

Some of the new recruits became ill from the hard work and bad conditions. Matt, accustomed to meager food and grateful to earn his passage, was a willing worker and Captain McDougall took notice of him, nodding his approval as he observed Matt working hard.

Only a few days out at sea, a storm struck the boat. Matt was thrown out of his bunk during the night, unable to get up. The floor seemed to be heaving up and down and other men were sprawled around him. The mate poked his head in the doorway shouting, "All hands on deck. A bad storm's blowing! Get going!"

With the ship pitching wildly, Matt and the other men stumbled and crawled up the steps. Thunder boomed over the water. Waves washed through the boat and over their faces, almost drowning the sailors clinging tightly to anything they could get their hands on. The ship dipped up and down like a teacup bobbing on the turbulent water. Matt felt like he was enveloped in deafening thunder that cracked without letup, lightening sparking from sky to water, threatening to set the boat on fire.

Fatigue set in and Matt's arms trembled. He began giving up hope. With a sinking feeling, he realized that nobody would know that he died. *Would Annie wonder why I haven't written?*

A monstrous wave roared over them. Matt saw a struggling sailor picked up and tossed over the side, disappearing instantly in swirling foam. Nothing could have saved him. Another big crack of thunder accompanied a tornado-like gale that sent the boat keening on one side. *The man in the Dungannon pub was not fooling when he said fierce winds blow up bad storms. Why didn't I pay attention?* Matt held on in terror. Shivering from the cold, arms weakening, Matt almost let himself slip down into the water. But thoughts of Annie's kiss forced him to wrap his arms firmly around the railing again. *Annie. Are you thinking of me? If I live through this, I'll write to you.*

Hours later, Matt hoped it wasn't his imagination that the squall was less violent. Every muscle in his body ached. His mouth was dry as cotton from the salt water he'd swallowed. When the waves had flattened enough to allow the men to loosen their grip and move around, Matt felt almost too weary to move. Exhausted, cold, and wet, Matt and the other sailors worked many hours to repair the damage from the storm. When he finally crawled into his hard bunk, he doubted that he'd ever see America.

Chapter 5

ARRIVING IN AMERICA
1888

"The Statue of Liberty!" Weeks after leaving the Old World, shouts resounded from the crew and a motley assortment of steerage passengers as the ship chugged past the renowned symbol of hope. Matt was too astounded to join in the cheering. As the realization that he'd actually sailed to America hit him, he exploded. Jumping into the air and tossing his cap sky-high, he whooped at the top of his lungs. "I made it to America!"

Amazed at the enormity of the churches, public buildings, factories, and other structures as they cruised into Hudson Bay, Matt stood staring. Busy as he was, Matt enjoyed the daybreak of this June morning in a New World as they cast anchor and waited for a tug to transport the emigrants to Manhattan's Castle Garden. Fascinated by the huge red granite fortress that served as the emigrant depot at Castle Garden, he asked Captain McDougall about it. The captain, who was instructing Matt on taking the passengers in to the reception area where they would be examined and inspected by immigration officials, told him that it had been built by the British in 1812. "They expected to rule this new colony when they came here to fight the War of Independence and built this big garrison to defend the harbor."

The landing dock was bustling with emigration officers. Matt led the mass of bodies from the landing dock, through a corridor, and into the building. After the immigrants received medical examinations, a staff of men in the center of the building began shooting questions at them, offering to help them with further arrangements. One man shouted: "Do you need to purchase tickets to travel on to another destination? Line up here."

Another yelled, "Do you want to find work or a place to board?" Men started racing to crowd in that area.

"Do you have money to exchange for American money?" Many immigrants had nothing left but pocket change. Only a few people stood in that line.

Since theirs was a freight ship, there were only poor steerage passengers who had paid $30 to sail across the ocean. Most of the needy passengers required a great deal of help. They also were in terrible need of some soap and baths, but none were available.

With the passengers in one big group, Matt realized that the majority of them were Irish. Few seemed to have money to travel past New York, although many were meeting a family member who had sent money back for their passage. Matt wondered what would happen to the men who were already destitute from paying for their passage.

The day before, Captain McDougall had stopped Matt to say, "You've worked hard. I have a good friend working on the docks, Mac McHale, and he could help you get a job. New York is the second biggest port in the world and good workers are needed. Would you be interested?"

"Thank you, sir. Sure, and I need a job desperately, I do."

Captain McDougall instructed Matt to return to the boat as soon as he was finished at Castle Garden. "There's lots of work to dock this ship and prepare it for its next journey. Mac McHale is usually at his favorite Irish pub on Washington Street. I'll take you to him after I finish my paperwork for Cooke Shipping Company." The Captain sent his list of passengers to the emigration officers, along with a request to speed up Matt's processing so he could get back to the ship.

It was nearly evening before all business with the Emigration Department was over. Most of the people remained in the big building to settle down on hard benches for the night. Matt was glad to be going back to the ship, away from the chaos of over-crowded quarters, the stench of unwashed bodies, and the cacophony of many different languages.

After everything on board was ship-shape and his work completed, Matt stood on deck watching all the activity in the magnificent harbor. Hudson River was swarming with steam tugboats pulling ships in and out, passengers disembarking, and baggage being loaded and unloaded. *'Tis too big here. I'll not stay long,* he promised himself.

Tiring of the noise and activity, he borrowed paper from the Captain and started a letter to Timmy, hoping it would get to him. After writing about his adventures in getting to America, he asked himself, *Should I write to Annie?* Touching his cheek as he remembered her kiss, he grabbed another sheet of paper. "Dear Annie . . ." Writing the endearment made him catch his breath, goose bumps rose on his arms as he wrote about his accomplishment.

> "Dear Annie: I made it to America! Our ship just docked in New York. We arrived at dawn and a lovely sunrise greeted me on my first day in the New World. It gave a rosy glow to the shoreline of this big city. Never have I seen such huge buildings, all built side by side. As soon as I got to Glasgow I found a ship sailing to America and worked for my passage. I thought I'd drown during a terrible storm. I saw another sailor get swept into the Atlantic Ocean by a huge wave. Thinking about you saved my life—it made me hold on tight. Captain McDougall is going to help me get a job on the docks unloading ships. I'll be leaving New York as soon as I save enough money to go searching for land."

Although it was late when Captain McDougall could finally leave the ship, he found his friend Mac McHale at the saloon. Mac agreed to take Matt to the docks. "I'm sure he'll get hired with your recommendation," he told the Captain as he took his note testifying that Matt was a good worker.

Mac turned to Matt. "Need a room? I'll take you to my boarding house. You can sleep on the floor beside my bed tonight; I can spare you a blanket. In the morning we'll talk to the lovely Freda Schneider to see if she has an empty bed. She'll make room for you, even if 'tis the floor. She could work on the docks herself, that one. Towering over us all, she turns us into cowards and keeps us in line."

"Where is the boarding house?"

"Lower East Manhattan, close to the waterfront. Most of the men living there are Irish, working on public works projects for meager wages. All the tenements there are miserable, but Freda tries a little harder than most landlords. She's a German widow and keeps the place pretty clean. Serves decent food, too." Matt squelched the urge to hug the man; instead, he breathed a prayer of gratitude. *Maybe it was that stop in Armagh that brought this bit of good luck.*

Chapter 6

NEW YORK CITY DOCK WORKER

1888-1889

Matt hated New York. "'Tis a stinking place, noisy and dirty, crowded with people and buildings," he told Mac. "The tall buildings block out the sky." He and Mac were wandering down Broadway, the main route for commerce. "'Tis almost instant death to try to cross this street. Look at all that traffic." Carriages, stage wagons, and drays rattled by, leaving no space for crossing at an intersection.

"Sure, and the noise so loud a man cannot think." The two men listened to horses' hooves clopping on cobblestones and the shouts of their drivers, the gongs and clanging of horse cars and streetcars, and the roar of the elevated train. Mounds of manure created an even worse experience for pedestrians. Matt watched a lady trying to cross the street, holding her skirt high with one hand and holding a lace handkerchief to cover her nose with the other.

Mac laughed. "Not the green of Ireland, is it now? Look over there at that big traffic jam. Nobody can move, they just sit there cussing. No, I'll not stay long in New York. How about you, Matt?"

"I'll be leaving the minute I have a bit of savings."

Coming home one night after an exceptionally busy day working on the docks in the rain, Matt's sagging spirits surged upward when Freda handed him a letter from Dungannon. He'd almost given up hope of getting a letter from Annie. He wasn't sure how long it took for letters to go back and forth, or if he could rely at all on the mail service.

His energy revived, Matt ran up the stairs to read Annie's letter. She sounded excited about hearing from him. Her last line said, "I'm looking forward to hearing from you again."

He ate supper quickly and went back to his room to write that he was settled in at Freda's boarding house, working hard on the docks, and had been exploring New York with his adventurous new friend, Mac. "I think there are more Irish here in Manhattan than in all of Ireland and they are not much better off. 'Tis poor they are here in America too. New York streets are filled with Irish newsboys, bootblacks, domestic servants running errands, Irish seamstresses going to or coming from work, and Irish laborers. There are some grand buildings, though."

As the months flew by, Matt began to wonder if anybody was left in the old country. How could there be? Each day, emigrants swarmed off the ships like ants finding something sweet. "Where do they all go?" he asked Mac.

Mac shrugged. "To the ghettos where they're stacked up like cordwood. German, Irish, Italian, Yiddish, Polish, Russian . . . The emigrants pretty much stay with their own people in their own areas."

As Mac had promised, Freda was a good landlady. Her toughness barely concealed her kind heart when she made homey little touches in the tenement. At Halloween, a smiling pumpkin glowed in the middle of the table.

It was the first Thanksgiving for most of the boarders and Freda offered to cook them a traditional American Thanksgiving meal if they wanted to contribute toward buying a turkey. They did. The men gathered at Freda's table looked at the bowls of food on the table and, without saying a word, crossed themselves and mouthed silent prayers. Before anybody left the table, Matt thanked Freda for the most delicious meal of his life. Other men mumbled their thanks before pushing away from the table, groaning that they had eaten too much.

Christmas in America was not a holiday for dock workers. Ships sailed into Hudson Harbor overflowing with emigrants as on any other day. However, Freda decided her tenants must enjoy a German Christmas. When they came home from work on Christmas Eve, they were surprised to see a small Christmas tree in the dining room. Freda had decorated it with a few precious ornaments she'd brought from Germany, her eyes sparkling with happiness in the light of the candles on the tree.

She served a delicious oyster stew for Christmas Eve. "Not a German supper, but a New York supper bought from Irish oyster men," she twinkled. As soon as their bowls were empty, she made them all sing the German carol, "O Christmas Tree." By the third round, her boarders were getting restless. Triumphantly she said, "I bring in German dessert." Nobody left the table when she ducked back into the kitchen. She came back with two plates and proudly held them up. "Lebkuchen and stollen." As quickly as the small spicy cakes and the fruit bread disappeared, the men disappeared too. Freda was content—she had her tree and had sung her favorite song.

Tired as Matt and Mac were, they could not allow Christmas Eve go by without going to Mass. *Faith, and I have so much to be thankful for,* Matt thought as he crossed himself while getting ready in his room. They bundled up to walk the few blocks to the Catholic Church where many Irish would be gathered to offer Latin devotions to the Virgin Mary and Baby Jesus. Although it was not far, the icy December wind was fierce and Matt was glad of the heavy coat Freda had managed to find for him. Since her boarders had little time to shop, she often found bargains for them, and Matt was grateful for her help.

When Matt and Mac came home from work on Christmas Day, they smelled the tantalizing aroma of roast goose. "This is a typical German Christmas dinner," Freda told them as she served the goose, applesauce, and potato dumplings. The Irishmen savored every bite.

Seated at the table, Freda praised Peggy and Rose Kennedy, two Irish sisters living at the boarding house. "They helped me pluck the goose and fix the dinner." Freda protected Peggy and Rose Kennedy like a mother hen. Matt treated them kindly, but occasionally a boarder made the mistake of flirting with them. Freda would stand threateningly over the culprit saying, "Ach. You keep away from them or you will be thrown out of my house."

Coming from Ireland's County Cork a few months ago, fifteen-year-old Peggy, and Rose, a year younger, had sailed all alone to America. At Castle Garden, Labor Department officials had gotten them jobs as sewing-machine hands in a garment factory. The sisters were excellent seamstresses, but they came home at night exhausted after working twelve-hour days in the sweatshop. "Conditions are bad. We are not allowed to talk at all, not at all. In twelve hours, we are given only one short break. The shorter our break, the more we can sew." Matt was amazed they were able to keep their sense of humor. He heard them giggling in their room at night. Most of their money was sent home to help support their parents and younger brothers and sisters. "Someday we will bring them all here," Peggy told Matt.

In January, seven months after arriving in New York, Matt decided it was time for a decent suit. In Ireland, men who wore suits were known to be good providers. He still remembered how the O'Brian manager, Kelly, would strut around in his suit on Sundays. Kelly knew how handsome he looked; he was muscular without an ounce of fat and with curly black hair. He'd brag, "All respectable Irishmen wear suits. It shows you are an honorable man, not gambling and drinking your money away." As a young boy, Matt had hoped to own a suit and look respectable one day. Now in America, he'd been carefully saving his money and it was time to buy that suit. He told Freda, "Sure, and I'll soon be leaving New York. Before I go I want to attend Mass at the grand St. Patrick's Cathedral."

Freda agreed that a suit was needed for such a visit. "This is a suit you will own for your whole life. It has to be a good one." She advised him to visit the garment district. "There are lots of sweatshops producing suits in the garment district. Go to Orchard Street. There are pushcarts on Orchard Street with bargain prices. But you have to haggle. Look the clothes over, find things wrong with them. Make a pitiful offer, then walk away. They'll come after you."

Matt shook his head. "'Tis not my way to cheat a man."

Freda said, "Ach, I will come with you." She jerked off her apron and grabbed her purse. On Orchard Street, she pawed through merchandise in pushcarts while haggling and shouting at the peddlers. She walked away in disgust, dragging Matt by the arm.

"I take you to a good tailor, Julius. Julius is a landsman-owner, he has his own store. This business starts with peddling from a sack on your back, then to a pushcart, and then the good businessman—to a real store. Julius worked hard to become a landsman-owner with his own store."

She led Matt into a shop barely wider than the door they'd walked through. A gray-bearded man wearing glasses sat in a corner hunched over a sewing machine. He jumped up as soon as he saw Freda. "Oy, Freda" was all that Matt could understand. He and Freda carried on a rapid conversation in German before she turned to Matt. "This is Julius. He came from Germany on the same boat as my husband and me. My husband Edward bought suits from Julius. He's a good tailor. Not like that shoddy stuff in the pushcarts."

Julius scrutinized Matt before pulling out a black suit from under a large pile. Julius held up the jacket, motioning Matt to try it on. The jacket fit perfectly, but he could tell the pants were too long. Freda rapidly spoke German to the stooped tailor. They argued for some time, Freda gesturing widely, and at one point she walked to the door.

Julius ran after her. "No, no, Freda." Freda glowered at him from the door, but walked back for further negotiating.

Finally Freda turned to Matt with a satisfied grin. "It's settled. You will buy this one. Pay Julius ten dollars."

Matt cringed. He had not intended to pay that much for a suit. He said, "But the pants are too long."

"I fix," Freda said. "The jacket fit well."

Matt had looked at some of the suits on the pushcarts and, although he knew nothing about tailoring, he could tell that the workmanship was poor. Julius's suit jacket felt like it had been made for him. Matt shrugged his shoulders and took out ten dollars.

Julius wrapped the suit in newspaper, all the while shaking his head and repeating, "Oy, Freda." Handing the wrapped suit to Matt, the little tailor said, "Good suit. Enjoy."

Walking back to Freda's with his package, Matt said, "I have no money left for a shirt."

"I have a shirt for you."

Freda hemmed the pants and when she gave them to him she also gave him a shirt. "My husband's," she said. "Edward wore this shirt only a few times before he died."

Matt took one look and said, "Too big."

The next evening, Peggy and Rose were busily cutting the shirt apart. They cut the pieces down to fit him and then sewed them together again. Peggy and Rose stood by grinning when Freda handed him the shirt, now freshly laundered and with a tie on top of it. "My Edward no longer needs tie or shirt," Freda said with tears in her eyes.

Wearing his new suit, he ventured to Fifth Avenue and 50th Street on a trolley early on a Sunday morning. Standing at the back of the immense Cathedral, he breathed in awe, *Faith, and I thought St. Patrick's in Armagh was grand.* His new clothes did not prevent him from feeling uncomfortable and out of place in such elaborate surroundings. He was content to have enjoyed the majestic Mass once in his lifetime. The next morning he told Mac, "From now on I'll attend Mass with the other Irish at the shabby church in our neighborhood, but this will be a memory to keep forever. And I'll have my new suit to keep forever."

Chapter 7

PENNSYLVANIA COAL MINER
1889-1892

Over a pint at a pub on the waterfront, Mac had heard that workers were badly needed in Pennsylvania. "John, the man who told me about it, is from the Labor Department of the Commissioners, he helps emigrants find employment. Agents from Pennsylvania are recruiting as many as they can for Pennsylvania lumber, coal, iron, and oil industries. He'll send an agent to us next time one shows up from Pennsylvania."

An agent found them on the docks a few days later. "John from the Labor Department at Castle Garden told me about you fellows. I'm Arthur Deutschberg from Pennsylvania." He told them that a man named Charlemagne Tower had acquired land in the Schuylkill Valley in Pennsylvania after accumulating a small fortune during the Civil War. "Now he's struck coal and is looking for coal miners. Wages are good. Pennsylvania miners have been organizing and striking for better pay for a few years now. He even built a new town and it's named after him—Tower City. It's located on Wiconisco Creek and surrounded by forests and mountains." Mr. Deutschberg paused to let that sink in. "Care to get out of these unhealthy slums, boys?"

Matt and Mac did not have to be coaxed. They drew the pay that was owed them and paid Freda their rent. Peggy and Rose had tears in their eyes when they said goodbye to them.

Surprisingly, Freda was upset that they were leaving. "My two best boarders. You should not leave until the St. Patrick's Day parade. That is your Irish holiday, you should be here. For many years, the Irish have been parading defiantly through New York streets, you could be with them."

Mac said, "Yes, we'll miss our Irish parade. But I also remember the blizzard we had in March after the big parade last year. The *New York Times* wrote that it was the worst storm the city has ever known. Remember that, Freda? The whole city was paralyzed with twenty-two inches of snow. We'll be leaving before any more March blizzards."

Arthur Deutschberg met them at the New York Central and Hudson River Railroad Depot. He purchased their tickets plus six more for the crew he'd gathered, immigrants freshly off a ship from Scotland. "These men are coming to Tower City to work in the coal mine too." He led them to a railroad car, seating everybody closely together. "The train will take us to Harrisburg, and then we'll travel by horse and wagon to Tower City."

On the train ride, Agent Deutschberg sat with Matt and Mac. He told them that his parents had settled in Pennsylvania after emigrating from Germany. "I've lived in Harrisburg all my life," he said. "Harrisburg became the state capital in 1812, which stimulated industrial development. During the Civil War the first concentration camp for Union forces was established here and named Camp Curtin in honor of the governor. Robert E. Lee's army had almost invaded the city, but for some unknown reason decided not to invade Susquehanna Valley and turned back. We felt the effects of the economic depression, but things are better now. Harrisburg has grown and now has a population of about 25,000."

The boarding house was stuck in with a bunch of identical small row houses provided for coal miners, but it was only ten years old and located on a pretty street with trees. Julia Fillner, her hair in a bun wound tightly on top of her head, reminded Matt and Mac of

Freda with her dominating ways as she told them her rules. Her husband was a coal miner and Julia ran the boarding house. Matt was barely settled in his room before sitting down to write to Annie so she would know where to send her next letter. He'd discovered by now that it took a letter about a month to reach its destination.

Matt hated being imprisoned down in the blackness of the mine and leaving at night covered with coal dust. Mac soon started courting a Deutschberg daughter and seemed content, but a Pennsylvania coal mine was not part of Matt's dream. Tower City was built on marshland; it was not the farming land Matt was searching for.

Two years later, Matt said goodbye to his friend Mac—who had already gotten a promotion into an office job—and his new little family. In his black New York suit made by Julius, he'd acted as best man when Mac married Hilda Deutschberg. A year later, Hilda produced a handsome son they named Matthew and the proud godfather wore his black New York suit for the christening.

Working at odd jobs along the way, Matt traveled on to Ohio. From Ohio he wrote:

"Dear Annie: I left Tower City and the coal mines and came further west to Ohio. Before leaving, I became godfather to Mac and Hilda's son, Matthew. They named him after me. There's good land in the Ohio Valley along the Ohio River, but it's heavily populated and expensive. Too expensive for me. I've heard that out West it's possible to get land for almost nothing. That's about all I can afford, so I'll probably keep going soon as I save more money."

Chapter 8

MINNESOTA COAL MINER
1892-1893

In 1892, the American economy was spiraling downward with unemployment increasing. Matt continued working at odd jobs until he found a permanent job pounding rails for a railroad yard in Steubenville, Ohio.

Matt heard rumors that land was pretty cheap up north. His desire to continue West was rekindled when he read an advertisement posted in the depot. The Minnesota Iron Company wanted to recruit experienced miners for its Mesabi Mine operation on the Iron Range. He was startled to see that the Mesabi Mine was owned by Charlemagne Tower, the same Philadelphia millionaire who owned the mine at Tower City. Checking into it further, Matt learned that Mr. Tower owned the train that brought the ore from Two Harbors to the iron and steel factories in Ohio. A settlement near the mines on the Mesabi Range was named Tower in the landowner's honor. *Must be a lucky sign. This same businessman has two towns named after him. Sounds successful.* Matt wasted no time in heading west.

Taking the train to Chicago, Matt purchased a ticket on the North-Western Line going to Duluth, Minnesota. Asking directions in the Duluth depot, he was told that Tower was about thirty miles away. *No need to take a train,* Matt thought. He walked the distance easily.

Because of his mining experience in Pennsylvania, he was hired immediately. "The town of Tower in Minnesota is named after the same man as Tower City in Pennsylvania," Matt wrote to Annie. "Faith, two towns named after only one man. Sure, I heard he was a Civil War leader, but I don't know how he made so much money that he can buy mountains filled with coal and iron ore!"

While working in Minnesota, Matt learned that the son of Charlemagne Tower who, like his father, was a Harvard graduate and a lawyer, had lived in Duluth for five years while he served as president of the Duluth and Iron Range Railroad. Tower had already returned to Philadelphia by the time Matt arrived.

The "Panic of 1892" grew into the "Depression of 1893" and unemployment became rampant in 1894. Talk about the mines not doing well increased, and whispers began circulating that miners would lose jobs. Then, buzzing started about the discovery of gold up north.

"A gold rush!" The rumors at Mesabi Mine intensified. Matt ignored them at first, but every day there were new reports about the big gold strike on an island near Canada. Miners were talking about rushing north. North-Western Railroad wanted more business and Rainy Lake City wanted more prospectors so they fed the frenzy with ads in **The Rainy Lake Journal:** "Why go to Alaska when gold can be found along the northern border of Minnesota?"

Matt discussed the exciting news with his friend, Mike McGuire. Matt's first day of work at the mine, he had been paired with Mike. Built like a barrel and powerful as an ox, Mike set a fast pace, but Matt was able to keep up with him. Immediately, Mike had invited him to share his room at the boarding house. "A pleasant widow lady runs it. Her husband was killed in a mine explosion and she needs the money. She'll be glad to have us share the room—it means she can collect double." Although he was another Irishman quite fond of his drinks, Matt enjoyed Mike's sense of humor. After he got to know him better, he said, "You must have kissed the blarney stone for sure." Mike got into many fistfights in the saloons, but usually came out the winner.

The more they read about the gold found in the north, the more they itched to go. Mike said, "A gold rush! We Irish are always looking for a crock of gold!"

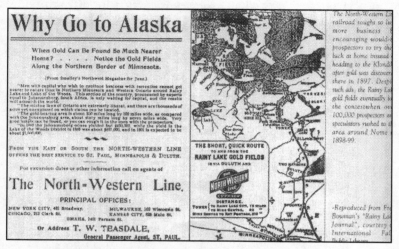

(-Reproduced from Gold Town to Ghost Town, p. 14,
with permission of Voyageurs National Park)

After reading the newspaper article, *Why Go to Alaska*, Matt said without hesitation, "Let's go! I heard that the streets in the next village of Koochiching are being paved in gold."

They argued over transportation. Mike wanted to go by train. "The railroad offers services from Duluth to Rainy Lake City. That sounds good to me."

Matt disagreed. "I'm not going all the way back to Duluth to pay $7.90 for a ride on the train. The newspaper claims there's a 'short, quick route' by the Tower Road. It's only fifty miles to Rainy Lake City. I walked a lot further than fifty miles when I left Ireland!"

The next night at the supper table, Mike said, "I heard you can get rides on wagons pulling supplies to the gold mine."

"Bouncing on a buckboard over bumpy roads doesn't appeal to me," Matt said. "I'm walking."

On March 15, 1894, Matt read in **The Vermillion Iron Journal:**

> Nine team loads of supplies bound for Rainy Lake City. The greater amount of the loads is composed of lumber, feed and flour. P.O. Slethem hauling 5 tons of general merchandise to Rainy Lake City to open up a general store."

Matt told Mike, "The paper said they're hauling lots of supplies to Rainy Lake City. The rumors must be true. 'Tis time to go. Let's pick up our pay tonight and leave tomorrow morning. The ice will be melting if we wait any longer."

Dressed in layers of warm clothes on a cold March morning, Matt and Mike joined the gold rush.

Chapter 9

ROAD TO GOLD

1894

Icy needles pelted his face. Ireland had blustery winds, but Matt had never known anything like the wind that whipped across the open expanse of ice in Minnesota. He worried that he would collapse without ever getting to Rainy Lake City. Cold gusts pushed at him, making it almost impossible to walk. Matt wished he had never left Tower. *Sure, and why did I leave that civilized town of Tower for this vast arctic wilderness? I'll freeze to death on this road to gold without ever finding my land.*

Turning his back to the wind, he warmed his face in his hands. Despite his misery, he suddenly laughed. He yelled to Mike, "'Twas just yesterday we wished for frigid temperatures when the sun was melting the ice at the dam. Sure, and we wanted it a wee bit cooler when we were walking through water on the ice, now didn't we?" Swift rapids with water opening up around Vermilion Dam forced them to walk cautiously, carefully checking the thickness of the ice.

Shivering, Mike said, "We should have waited for summer and traveled by water in a canoe."

"No, those canoes look too tippy for me. Better to depend on my own legs."

Stopping to catch his breath, Matt saw something in the distance. "What's up ahead? Maybe it's those hotels we heard about!" Entrepreneurs, realizing that hopeful travelers heading up north to get rich would pay for a bunk, had quickly thrown up shacks at Crane Lake Portage. With a spurt of energy, Matt walked faster. "Hurry up, let's see if we can get a bed for the night."

"'Tis the luck of the Irish, Mike," he said as they each paid a dollar for the last two bunks. He asked the innkeeper, "How much further to Rainy Lake City?"

The innkeeper answered, "Twenty-seven miles."

They devoured a meal with other hopeful prospectors rushing to the gold mines. An Irishman named Boston was bragging about all the gold he'd panned at Rainy Lake City. "I took it to Duluth to sell. I had a good time, but now I'm broke and going back for more." He'd blown his money on whiskey and women. "Enjoyed every minute!" he boasted to Matt.

Matt listened wide-eyed to Boston's exciting stories about his previous adventures panning for gold. He bragged, "I saw a big nugget of pure gold."

Matt and Mike decided it would be a good idea to link up with Boston the rest of the way to Rainy Lake City. When they approached him, Boston shrugged, "I won't turn down the company."

When Mike complained about the filthy blankets, Matt said, "The blankets are none too clean, but at least we're out of the snow and cold." Matt became more determined than ever to walk with Boston after observing other men taking off gun belts when they bunked down that night.

Matt barely closed his eyes all night for fear that Boston might leave without them. He daydreamed about Annie more than he slept. When he wasn't dreaming about Annie he wondered what that "Island of Gold" would be like. *Sure, and what would Timmy think, me going to find gold.* The minute the blanket over Boston moved, Matt poked Mike. They rolled out of bed, pulled on their boots, and were ready to go.

After gulping down a breakfast of half-cooked bacon and eggs fried in the bacon grease, Matt stood outside the wooden hotel watching the activity. Horses hitched to wagonloads of mining equipment stood snorting and stomping. A sleigh piled high with mail was ready to leave, the driver slapping the reins, trying to coax the horse to move. He nodded to Matt, "I hope it don't warm up too much. Last week I ran into some open water and thought I was going down with the sleigh. Lucky the horse got scared and made a run for it, got us across safely. This time of year can be risky—never know if temperatures will be freezing or thawing. I try to go on the ice road as long as I can. Going overland is much longer and full of potholes." The driver slapped the reins again and the horse trotted off.

Matt and Mike fell in behind Boston. While talking, Boston said his last name was O'Brien and looked none too pleased when Matt roared with laughter. He explained, "I left the O'Brians in Ireland because I hated them, and now here I am in America with another one." Boston laughed with Matt at the coincidence. "But 'tis is a common name."

Boston gave them good information about what to expect. "Bevier Mining owns the gold mine now. You go to work for them and they pay you monthly. The mining company pays the expenses and you won't have to starve to death while panning for gold."

Matt was relieved. "Sounds good to me." Matt didn't dream about becoming rich. Not that he would refuse it! He just wanted to earn enough money to buy a chunk of land. That was his dream when he left Ireland six years ago and time had not changed it. And to be freer of oppression and have the right to vote!

Matt told Boston, "I had to go to Scotland to get a visa because so many people are still fleeing from Ireland. Catholics haven't been able to own land or horses since Penal laws were first passed in 1695." Matt remembered that history lesson very well—when he'd learned about the English lords who had taken the land and their rights away from the Irish people. He'd never lost his anger.

Boston nodded. "Yeah. My grandparents fled Ireland in 1848 during the Potato Famine when Da' was a wee lad. They said people were falling dead from starvation on the streets of Donegal.

Life wasn't much better for my parents living in the Irish ghetto in Boston. That's where I was born, in the slums. We were dirt poor."

"People are still starving in Ireland. Prime Minister Gladstone tried to improve things with The Land Act of 1870, but it didn't help us any in Donaghmore. English landowners still treat their tenants badly," Matt informed him. "I could hardly wait to leave." Shaking his head in wonder he added, "I still can't believe I did it."

Between conversations, Annie Rice dominated Matt's thoughts as he trudged along in the cold. *Had she gotten his last letter? Did she still think about him?*

Chapter 10

RAINY LAKE CITY
1894-1896

"We're gettin' close! C'mon!" Boston hollered through the blizzard. Matt could barely pick up one foot after the other, he was so cold and weary. "There's a warm fire and a shot of whiskey just around that bend." Boston urged them to go faster. When the three men stumbled into Pat Roche's tent saloon, somebody shouted, "Boston, is that really you?"

Jeff Hildreth, the manager of Little American Mine, was in the saloon. "You old codger, ain't you dead? You don't think I'm going to hire a ghost, do you?"

Boston pulled coins out of pocket. "Still charging fifteen cents for a drink?" he asked Pat. "You bartenders are robbers!"

Taking a big gulp of beer, Matt told Hildreth that he and Mike had been working at Mesabi Mine and had read the newspaper reports about the gold discovery. "If you want to work, report to me first thing in the morning," the mine manager said as he finished his beer and left.

Matt soon discovered that the tent city was filled with men who flew into rages with very little to provoke them. Fascinating stories about lawless prospectors were told and re-told in the saloons. Matt was warned about Gold Bug Jimmie, who "salted" gold mines and sold them to gullible greenhorns new in town. Gold Bug would load a shotgun with gold flakes and powder and blast gold into a claim, fooling hopeful prospectors into thinking they would get rich quick.

There was another story about Patty the Bird, a prospector with a reputation as a barfly. "One day Patty the Bird stood in the middle of the street guzzling from a whiskey bottle. James Turney, a nice fellow except when he was drinking, decided to show off his expertise with a Colt 45 and shot the bottle out of Patty's hand. Patty howled when the glass splinters hit his face. He thought he'd been shot and fell down in a faint."

Matt eventually learned that the real reason Boston left Rainy Lake City was because Pat Corrigan, the owner of a saloon, shot him. According to the bartender telling Matt the story, "Boston and Dell Clark were drinking in the saloon when Boston suddenly shouted, 'I feel like killing somebody!' Knocking drinks to the floor, he began shooting at Corrigan. Boston barely missed Corrigan's head. Enraged, Corrigan chased the outlaws out of the bar with his gun, and then shot Boston in the cheek and throat. Boston was loaded up and taken to the town of Fort Frances across the Canadian border for medical treatment, but was expected to die." Matt now realized that people were disappointed to see that Boston had survived the shooting.

Matt discovered quickly that hard rock mining for gold was as strenuous as iron ore mining. In that raw mining town of only two hundred people, there were about a dozen tent saloons where the miners relaxed on their time off. Mike spent his time off in the saloons, but not Matt. Saloons would not get Matt's money. Knowing that the ice wouldn't last much longer, he was busy exploring the area. So far, his search for farmland had been futile on the rocky islands of Rainy Lake.

Temperatures seesawed through April into the first of May. Mother Nature teased with temperatures soaring into the 40's, creating slush and puddles, then plunging back down to freeze the lake solid again. Matt asked, "Does winter last forever here?" Other prospectors were weary of winter, too and they all wondered whether old-timers from the area meant it when they said, "We'll get a day or two of summer, don't you worry. 'Course, when it comes, the mosquitoes will carry you away!" Matt hoped they were joking.

Matt read in the **Rainy Lake Journal** that last year the ice had gone out April 25, but this year predictions were that it might not go out until mid-May. Despite the weather, Matt found Minnesota intriguing. He was mesmerized by the sounds as he traversed the lake. The first time he'd heard a booming that reverberated like cannon, he stopped dead still, wondering what he was hearing. "That's the ice expanding and contracting," he was told when he asked about the noise. Another time it rumbled as though from a giant stomach. He'd heard moaning and groaning that sounded as though animals were in pain. Whenever the ice sounds started, he stopped to listen.

The first Sunday in May he wanted to get to mainland and was gingerly picking his way on ice that looked solid, remembering Pat Roche's warning that the ice could not be trusted this time of year. Crack! Matt's leg plunged into icy cold water. Heart pounding, he pulled his leg out quickly and scrambled away on all fours. His frozen pants leg wrapped around his leg, making it even more difficult to walk. His frozen foot was numb before he got back to camp.

Wearily, he limped into Pat Roche's saloon and downed a whiskey to warm up. Pat helped him pull off his boot, a slow and painful process. When they finally got it inched off, Pat brought in snow to rub on Matt's foot. The foot throbbed as it thawed out. His boot still wasn't dry in the morning, and it never again fit right, causing blisters after a long day in the mines.

When the ice was gone and the waterway open, Matt borrowed a canoe from an Ojibwe Indian named King who worked at Rainy Lake City. Matt did not like the way some of the miners treated the Indians and made a point to be friendly. The thawing streets were a muddy mess and King had been hired with several other Indians; they were paid $2.00 a day to improve the muddy sidewalks. The Indian's full name was Way-We-Zhe-Quam-Aish-Kung. The miners shortened it to King.

King was a member of the Bois Fort Tribe in Canada, moving with other members of his tribe to the Sha Sha area, across from Rainy Lake City, when they heard about the gold rush.

King squatted on a piece of land in a cozy bay protected from the wind on the west shore of Black Bay. His teepee was snuggled against a high rock ridge on the east. A forest of pine trees grew on the north side, wherever good soil was available on the rocky land. Chokecherry trees, blueberries and raspberries grew abundantly on the rock ridge; the Indian women sold the berries to the white settlers at Rainy Lake City and the little village of Ranier located between Rainy Lake City and Koochiching. Wild roses and blue flags bloomed on the riverbank, orange Indian paintbrush and white daisies crept out of fissures in the rock. Grapevines wrapped around evergreen trees.

Glaciers had created rocky islands that met King's needs. There were rich resources that provided food: fish, deer, moose, and bear. He trapped beaver, mink, and otter for furs, and wore deerskin clothes and moccasins. Well-built with flowing long, black hair, King had an easy-going disposition and seemed to take no offense at the prospectors' teasing, and sometimes demeaning, remarks.

George Griswold, a teacher in the school at Rainy Lake City, told Matt, "The Ojibwe tribe was known as 'Sug-waun-dug-ah-wiun-e-wug.' In English, that means 'men of the thick fir woods.'" Pleased to have an adult interested in history, the teacher explained, "The Ojibwe apparently moved into Minnesota from the Eastern coast in the early 1700's when European settlers began coming to America and stealing their land. As the colonies and states grew, the Ojibwe fought their way west along the shores of the Great Lakes and into what became Minnesota. Possibly they had more guns, so they were able to drive the Cree and the Assiniboine out of Minnesota into northeastern North Dakota. Disease, harsh winters, and occasional periods of famine kept Ojibwe populations low. The entire Indian population of Minnesota never exceeded fifteen thousand."

Matt exclaimed, "That's not many people! No wonder they couldn't defend their land."

"Native Americans were already living among the huge forests of pines and firs on Rainy Lake when the voyageurs came through. Voyageurs were the early fur traders, following the Mississippi River, Lake Superior, and then to Rainy River. Fort St. Pierre on the Canadian side of Rainy River was built in 1731. I suppose you haven't had a chance to get over to the town of Fort Frances, Ontario, across the river?"

Matt said, "Nope. I heard that's the name of the town over there, though.

"Have you seen the rapids at Ranier?" George asked.

Matt shook his head. "Haven't been there either."

"Have King paddle you over there in his canoe. Those rapids are something. They became a gathering place for traders catching fish. The early inhabitants named it Kay-Nah-chi-Wah-Nung, which means "The Place of the Long Rapids."

Matt wrote:

"Dear Annie: You'd not believe the school here in the wilderness. George Griswold, the teacher, has started the first school in Koochiching County with sixteen students. He's teaching me about America, about the Indians who came after the glaciers left and then the early fur traders who came by water. It's hard to believe anybody would bring wives and children to this muddy island filled with men greedy for gold. Some of these prospectors have notorious pasts. Mining for gold is hard work, and whenever I get a day off, I search for land."

Matt and Mike McGuire planned to celebrate the Fourth of July together. They seldom saw each other now because Mike spent his free time in the tent saloons, but Matt refused to spend his hard-earned money on whiskey; his goal of buying land still consumed him. Frank J. Bowman, editor and owner of **Rainy Lake Journal** promised lots of excitement. Because of Bowman's publicity, boatloads of people from Koochiching and Fort Frances were coming to see a demonstration of the expensive new stamp mill purchased by the Little American Mining Company. Matt wondered if the little island could hold the crowds of people swarming onto it. He hoped it wouldn't sink.

Matt and Mike were as anxious as the crowds to find out how the new crushing mill worked. Extracting the gold ore from the quartz buried in rock was difficult, but Matt was amazed at how much heavy equipment was being purchased without concern about expenses. Although they had listened intently to the explanation of how the mill worked, Matt read the newspaper for more details:

> "The stamp mill, a common crushing facility of the time, works on the mortar-and-pestle principle. Ore, water and mercury are fed into a trough and heavy steel stampers (pestle), weighing 800 to 2000 pounds each, fall in a progressive fashion crushing the quartz into a fine pulp."

Matt thought Editor Bowman did a fine job of writing about the celebration and sent the *Journal* article to Annie. He knew that he'd never be able to describe the pride he felt in celebrating America's Independence Day as eloquently as Mr. Bowman, so he clipped out the article and sent it to Annie.

"July 4, 1894, will be long remembered by everyone so fortunate as to have been present here on that day. It will pass into history as the day on which Rainy Lake City proved to the world that she is something more than a mere mining camp and that her leading industry is something more than a mere fake gotten up to sell town lots. Her claims to patriotic enterprise are established and her importance as a commercial center will henceforth be recognized on every hand.

"At 2:00 the stamp mill was packed to the utmost by an eager, anxious crowd. The time for starting the stamp had come and everybody was intent on seeing the first operations. Jeff Hildreth's face wore a confident but anxious look. Capt. West was calm and serene as usual . . . Col. Geggie tried to look happy and actually succeeded. Capt. West turned on the steam and George S. Davis . . . shoveled in the first ore. Every part of the machinery worked to a charm."

Despite the Fourth of July speeches, the bullion produced by the mill did not cover expenses and the Little American Mine kept sinking further into debt. Worried about how long he'd have a job, Matt scrimped even more to save money.

Chapter 11

THE HOMESTEAD
1896-1910

The ice was completely out of Rainy Lake on May 16th and Matt asked King to give him a ride in his canoe over to the mainland. He packed up a sleeping bag and some food and caught a ride on a wagon going to the village of Koochiching. He camped a few miles out of the village and the next morning continued traveling west along Rainy River. Following a creek into a heavily forested area, he stopped to scoop up a fistful of the earth now and then. He worked the soil in his hand, sniffing it until he could almost taste the dirt. This was the gold he was after—LAND!

His heart pounded as he paced out a large area that appeared to be fertile enough for farming, although it was covered with trees that would have to be cut down. He hammered a stake into the ground, hoping nobody else had filed a claim for it under the Homestead Act of 1862. It didn't take him long to cover the five miles back to the village of Koochiching.

Back at camp, he found the mining superintendent. Excitedly, Matt told Jeff Hildreth, "I need some time off to get to the claim office. I found a piece of land and want to stake my claim before somebody else files for it." After filing his claim, Matt visited his land as often as he could.

Goldville. The name for his homestead popped into his head as he paced his land. The name Goldville would be a reminder that he found the land he'd dreamed of when he was lured to Koochiching by gold. *I'll name the creek Gold Creek. Sure, and maybe someday I'll find gold on my own land! 'Tis a lucky name, I know it.*

Watching the Little American Mine become swamped by problems, Matt was glad that he'd found his land. Gold was not easy to extract from the quartz veins and needed huge equipment, engineers, and a big labor force. The overhead was crippling the mining companies. Some miners had already left for another gold rush in Alaska.

One night the miners in Pat Roche's bar heard somebody yelling, "Robbers, robbers!" They all ran out of the bar. Mr. Butler, who owned the bank, kept yelling that thieves had knocked him to the floor and stolen all the money from his safe. A big search party scoured the woods for the robbers, but not a trace was found of them.

When the search party wearily came back, they discovered that Mr. Butler had made a hasty departure. The sheriff and a posse quickly set out after him, catching the banker at Kettle Falls. They brought him back to Rainy Lake City and forced him to pay his customers their money. Mr. Butler insisted he wasn't escaping, he'd gone to get money so he could pay everyone back.

Panic became worse after the bank robbery. In spite of the optimistic tone of the **Rainy Lake Journal,** rumors that the mines were on the skids escalated.

The summer of 1896, efforts were made to revitalize the mine, but the gold was trickling out. An incompetent worker let $10,000 in gold run through the processing mill into the lake, and another time, a dock collapsed and the season's entire production of ore was dumped into 30 feet of water.

Matt decided it was time for him to leave. Under the 1862 Homestead Act, he had to have proof of five years of residency to file on a maximum of 160 acres. Continually worried that somebody else might try to grab his land, he quickly built a one-room log cabin to "prove" his claim. Matt knew he would not stop feeling uneasy about his claim until he actually held the U.S. Patent in his hands.

Matt stared at the signature. He could hardly believe that the document he held in trembling fingers proved that he owned the land. The U.S. Patent, received five years after he'd filed his claim, was signed by President William McKinley and dated November 28, 1900.

He remembered the vow he'd made as he marched past the O'Brian castle that May morning in Ireland. It was a long and arduous journey, but he was now a landowner in America! President McKinley himself gave his authority for him to own the land. Clutching the patent and grinning, Matt paced across his cleared fields. As he had done when he saw the Statue of Liberty, he tossed his hat into the air, shouting, "This land belongs to me!" Matt startled himself with his joyous shout, and he laughed out loud when he saw the white tails of three deer skittering into the forest.

Looking at the precious document again, Matt thought, *Sure, and I have to write Annie.* But first, he found a safe place to hide his deed.

> "Dear Annie: I've just received the best Christmas gift of my life from himself—the President of the United States! He signed the paper proving this land is mine. I named it Goldville! This land is my gold. I stopped working at Rainy Lake City and have been cutting down trees to clear my land, getting it ready for farming."

Lying in bed that night Matt reminisced about his journey: Timmy's tears that made him feel guilty for leaving; the storm at sea when he thought he would drown; working in mines in Pennsylvania and various jobs in Ohio; the bitterly cold walk to Rainy Lake City and toiling in the gold mine. His expedition had been rigorous, but his freedom was worth it.

The years flew by, but Matt didn't rest. Winters, he cut down trees; summers, he tilled the black dirt and planted gardens. As the townspeople in the village of Koochiching heard about his produce, they came out to his farm to buy cabbages and carrots, corn and potatoes. Then he bought chickens and sold fresh eggs.

With his small farm business flourishing, he bought a cow and started selling milk to a few people. Next, he decided he needed a horse. Taking his time, he looked at several horses before finding a strong work horse. *My horse and I will have lots of work do on the homestead; I need the best I can find.* Wistfully, he thought about Timmy. He'd written to Timmy a few times, but had never received a reply. *Faith, what would Timmy say if he knew I bought a horse. And what would the OBrians and their arrogant manager, Kelly, think of that?* Laughing out loud, he told his new horse, Kate, "Sure, and they would never believe it. It's a long ways I've come."

His next project was to build a log barn for his animals. Digging out his axe and hand saw, he began felling trees. In the spring, the entrepreneur added a new product to his egg and milk route—water. His inventory of goods to sell to the growing population in the village was also growing.

After delivering milk and eggs, he scrambled down the banks of Rainy River to fill barrels with water. His customers paid twenty-five cents for each barrel of water. After selling his products, he went back home to log more land, clearing it to plant hay and grain to feed his livestock. A larger house replaced his crude one-room cabin; it had a roof and floor made from lumber cut on George Miller's portable sawmill powered by a steam engine. Matt was living the dream he'd had when he left Ireland, the dream of owning his own small estate. It had taken hard work and perseverance, but he never regretted leaving the miserable existence in Ireland. He loved walking around his property, hands clasped behind his back, amazed himself at how much he had accomplished. Busy expanding his homestead and achieving the goals of a young Irishman, he'd disregarded another aspect of his life. A family.

A frosty Christmas Eve awakened Matt to the isolation of his life. Carrying pails of fresh milk from the barn, Matt stood in the early winter dark, listening. Wolves were howling. The towering forest closing in on him appeared menacing and he felt utterly alone in the world. Loneliness penetrated his bones. Shivering more from despair than the cold, he shuffled to his log house.

He missed Annie's letters. *Why had she stopped writing? Had she gotten married?* It was a lonely Christmas as he realized how solitary his life had become.

For several days, thoughts of Annie and the notion of marriage nagged at him as he hacked out stumps, tended his cows, and marketed his products. Finally, Matt sat down to write a letter to Annie.

"Dear Annie: I'm really lonesome and miss your letters. I know I waited a long time to tell you this, but I've been so busy working on my farm I didn't notice how the years were flying by. I never stopped thinking about you, though. Annie, if you're not married, would you welcome me if I came back to visit you? You often told me in your letters how disgusted you were with your brothers and that you were tired of running the family store. Long ago, you told me you dreamt about America too. Do you think you would want to come back with me?"

The next morning, after deliveries, Matt drove to Third Street and stopped in front of the post office. He sat in his wagon, staring at the letter, worrying about what he should do. *Should I mail it or not?* Jumping off the wagon before he could change his mind, he darted inside and shoved the letter into the slot. Staring at the empty slot, his knees buckled and he leaned against the wall for support. *I've waited too long! I know I've waited too long! She's forgotten me.*

As Matt stumbled out of the post office, John Lawrence was coming out of his pharmacy next door. Looking at Matt he asked, "Matt, are you okay? You look pale."

Matt replied, "Oh, just working too hard, I guess."

Each day Matt worried, *Will Annie answer?*

Matt could not stand the suspense. Before his letter had time to reach Annie, he packed up his New York black suit made by Julius and left for Ireland.

Section II

Irish Correspondence

Chapter 12

ANNIE'S STORE

Dungannon, Ireland 1888-1910

Annie stood in her doorway watching Matt walk down the street. Fate had brought him from Donaghmore into her little produce store; minutes later, she was feeling a sense of loss as fate took him away. Thinking about the impulsive kiss she'd just given a man leaving Ireland forever, she felt herself blush. Silently she begged, "Please write to me, Matt."

When Barbara, Annie's favorite sister-in-law, came into the store, Annie blurted out the story of the encounter: "Sure, and wasn't I sitting behind the counter sewing when the door banged. It startled me and I dropped my spool of thread. The stranger and I both ran to pick it up and we bumped heads. When we stood up, we were eye-to-eye, he was that short. But handsome with black curly hair."

"You bumped heads! That means you'll be marrying the man!"

"That's just an old Irish superstition!" Annie sputtered, her milky-white skin turning pink. "How can I marry him? He's on his way to America." Normally a feisty sixteen-year-old, Annie's body slumped. Head bowed, she murmured, "I'll not see him again."

While working in the store, Annie tried to imagine Matt's journey. Each day she wondered how far he'd gotten. *Did he get to Glasgow? Did he find a ship? Had he landed safely in America?* Two months later, the postman delivered a letter from America. Annie held the letter over her pounding heart before ripping open the envelope.

"Dear Annie . . ." *He said dear Annie!*

Annie ran for stationery. "Dear Matt . . ." Matt answered her quickly, telling about his experiences in New York. Her heart still leaped at the greeting when she saw "Dear Annie."

"Dear Annie: I'm all settled in here in New York. My new friend Mac helped me get a job on the docks and a room in his boarding house. Freda rules the boarders, who are mostly Irish, with an iron fist. Mac is an adventurous man and I've ridden on trolleys with sparks flying overhead and a train called an El on high stilts above the city. New York is crowded with people and high buildings close together. I plan to visit St. Patrick's Cathedral as soon as I can buy decent clothes. I hear 'tis a grand cathedral that took twenty years to build. I stopped to pay my respects to our Patron Saint at St. Patrick's Cathedral in Armagh on my way to Dungannon, now I hope to pay him my gratitude at another grand St. Patrick's Cathedral in New York City."

Annie's mother, Susan, overheard Barbara teasing Annie about the letters. They were seated around the table at a traditional Sunday dinner with all the family. Susan demanded to hear the entire story. Annie glared at Barbara before explaining to her mother about meeting Matt when he came in to buy an orange.

With a wicked gleam in her eye, Barbara said, "They bumped heads."

A staunch believer in Irish superstition, Susan said. "I forbid you to write to that man."

"Ma, his letters are so interesting. From Glasgow, Matt worked out his passage on a ship sailing to America. During a bad storm he almost drowned. Now he's working on the docks in New York, but he intends to own land someday."

"Are you not too young to be writing to somebody I've never met? And him off to a foreign land?"

"But, Ma, he's a Catholic. He stopped at St. Patrick's Cathedral in Armagh to pay his respects before leaving Ireland and now he plans to visit the grand new St. Patrick's in New York."

"I forbid you to write. I'll not hear another word from you."

Susan Rice liked to have her family around her and definitely would not consider letting a daughter move to America. Susan had battled ferociously when her older daughter Minnie told her that her husband Thomas had taken a job in Scotland, which was just across the Irish Sea. Susan had forbidden them to leave.

Thomas refused to change his mind. Stubbornly resisting all efforts by his mother-in-law, and then his wife when she succumbed to her mother's bidding, he said, "Do you see me with a job in Ireland? How can I support us? I can get work in Scotland. We will move."

Bravely as he had endured the shouting and tears over the move, he and Minnie were unable to say no to Susan's increased wailing about taking her grandson away. A wee toddler, Frank was left with his grandma. With Susan's failing health, Annie bore most of the responsibility for Frank's care. Not that she minded. As the years passed, Annie considered Frank a son. Sighing, Annie realized she'd never be able to leave Frank behind even if Matt wanted her to marry him. "'Tis for the best that we don't write," she admitted to Barbara.

Six months after Susan's decree, Annie told her mother, "You had no need to worry. He's not written again." She walked around the store with a heavy heart.

But a letter arrived from Pennsylvania shortly after that statement to her mother. Annie was too excited to remember her mother's command not to write. *What a brave man, daring to leave New York for an unknown destination! I have to answer him!*

With long intervals between letters, the correspondence continued. Annie came close to spilling the secret when Matt wrote about such an interesting event that she began talking about it at a Sunday gathering. She had never heard anything about the American

Indians helping people in Ireland until Matt wrote about it. "My friend Mac told me that way back when the Irish were starving from the potato failure, the Choctaw Indians sent money and food during the Irish Famine in the 1850's. They lived in the Great Plains of America and had barely enough to eat themselves, but they were the only people that sent food to Ireland during the Great Famine."

At the Sunday dinner table she asked, "Did you know that Indians in America sent food and money to Ireland during the Great Famine?"

Everybody stared at her. Frowning, Susan gave her an icy glance. "And where did you hear such a story?"

Annie, realizing her mistake, stammered, "Well . . . Well . . . 'Tis a story I read somewhere."

Her brother James, who hoped to immigrate to America himself some day, quickly interceded, "I've heard the story. Sure, and they were the only people who ever bothered with the poor starving Irish dropping dead on their streets. A million Irish died, but nobody cared." James winked at Annie from across the table. Annie gave him a grateful smile, hoping he would continue keeping her secret.

Luckily, young Frank demanded Grandma Susan's attention just then with a tantrum. Barbara was trying to force him to eat the peas he was willfully pushing off his plate onto the floor. Annie breathed a sigh of relief as the conversation turned to other topics while Susan tended to Frank.

Annie could hardly contain her happiness whenever she received a letter. Sometimes her mother would ask, "Sure, and why are you so happy today?" Fortunately, whenever the postman came Susan was taking a nap. She suffered from Bright's disease, and only felt well enough to work in the store for a short time. The swelling from the kidney disease had forced her to become a semi-invalid. Being on her feet aggravated the swelling.

On this day, Annie had run out for a quick errand and Susan said she would stay a few minutes longer until she got back. Annie was delayed and the postman delivered a letter from America. Susan angrily waved the letter the second Annie stepped through the door. "'Tis a letter from America. You disobeyed me!"

"Ma, his letters are so interesting and exciting. He worked in mines in Pennsylvania, then on a railroad in Ohio, and now he's in Minnesota."

"Do I want my daughter scalped by Indians?"

"Ma, I'm not marrying him, just writing."

"You heard me, Annie."

Another letter arrived. Annie gasped in disbelief as Matt shared his latest adventure:

> "Dear Annie: I'm working in a gold mine in northern Minnesota. 'Twas a long walk to Rainy Lake City—fifty miles over a frozen lake and bitterly cold—but my friend Mike McGuire and I joined a gold rush. We met an Irish fellow named Boston going back to the mine and walked with him. There are lots of wild prospectors here. Turns out Boston is one of the worst, but he got us here safely."

Annie tried to ignore the letter, but the thought of not corresponding made her despondent. She justified—*we'll never see each other again*—as she scribbled an answer.

Although Susan suspected that Annie still wrote to Matt, her steadily declining health had forced her to become completely bedridden. The disease progressed quickly, shutting down her kidneys. Knowing she was on her deathbed, but still determined to prevent her daughter from leaving Ireland, she pleaded, "Promise me you will never write to that man. I'll not go to my grave worrying if my daughter is going to get killed by an Indian."

Annie promised.

The wake was a big affair. Susan's customers came to pay their respects to the shrewd businesswoman who had managed to raise her family by working hard. Annie listened to the comments as friends, neighbors and customers filed past the coffin. "'Tis sad, only 52 years old. Young Frank will miss his Grandma. He loved her so much, he didn't go to Scotland when his mother left. Will Annie be able to take care of Frank and the store all alone?"

Busy with the store and raising Frank, Annie had little time to grieve. When a letter from Matt arrived, she went to her priest. She knew Susan had confided how opposed she was to Annie's correspondence with an unknown man in America. Aware of the promise Annie had made at her mother's deathbed, he said, "You cannot break the promise you made to your mother on her deathbed, can you now? Would you be able to forgive yourself such a sin?" Forcing herself not to write, Annie's heart ached. Matt's letters slowly stopped coming.

Several years later, Annie rejoiced with Matt as she read the news he couldn't resist sharing: "I bought land. I'm a landowner! I've built a log cabin from my own trees." His dream had come true.

Annie desperately longed to share Matt's excitement. Again, she rushed to her priest. Pious Father Michael said severely, "Can you in all conscience break that promise your mother asked you to make?"

Annie continued running the produce store for her family, hating it more each year, and dragging herself through the dismal days.

Chapter 13

A SHORT ENGAGEMENT

Annie's brother, James, stopped at the store one evening to tell Annie he was going to America. "My friend, Liam—you remember Liam, the one you said was too bold and boisterous—he wants me to help him run an Irish pub in New York. He says his saloon in the Bronx is a popular place for the Irish in New York City. 'Tis an opportunity I cannot turn down. With Ma gone, I can finally leave Ireland."

Angrily she shouted, "I stopped writing to Matt because Ma demanded it on her deathbed. If she had known you'd be running off, she'd have made you promise too! Now I've lost Matt and you are free to go!"

Trying to soothe her, James invited her to go to Tyholland with him when he went to say good-bye to their Rice relatives. "Maude and I will be going on Saturday. Have your friend, Maggie, run the store and you come with us. 'Twill do you good to get away."

Furiously she yelled, "I want nothing to do with you!"

She brooded for two days, sinking deeper into depression. It was an effort to get up in the morning and she lost all interest in the store. When James came to ask her again, she said yes, hoping it might cure her melancholy. Annie daydreamed about Matt on the day-long trip. As they passed pretty whitewashed cottages with thatch roofs, cows and sheep grazing on the lush green fields, she wondered, *Does Matt's farm look like that? Everything in Ireland is built from stone—what would a log cabin look like?*

They stayed with their uncle, Edward Ross Rice, and his wife, Katherine. On Sunday morning they went to Mass in the charming old church built in 1827. Annie stood in front of the altar looking up reverently at the two beautiful stained glass windows. The white marble altar was centered between the windows. A brass plate under the left window read, "Erected by Louie B. Rice in memory of his deceased sisters." The left window was dedicated "in memory of his deceased brothers." Her own relatives honored with stained glass windows! She felt a sense of peace as she gazed at them in awe.

Aunt Katherine introduced Annie to a dapper looking man with a mustache as they stood visiting in the churchyard. Daniel held her hand longer than he should have and followed them as they walked to their horse and wagon. He told Annie, "I'll be in Dungannon on business in a couple weeks. Could I come visit you?"

Annie thought about Daniel on the way home. He wasn't as handsome as Matt, but he was taller and nicely dressed in a suit. *Well, we'll see if he shows up.*

A few weeks later Annie looked up to see Daniel standing in the store. Although she gave him a tongue lashing for taking his time to come for a visit, he glibly offered excuses and stayed at the store until she practically shoved him out the door when she got busy. Annie confided to Barbara, "A gift of gab he has, but there's something about him I don't like. He acts arrogant and sneaky."

Barbara wasted no words. "Wake up, Annie. You haven't heard from Matt for over a year. Daniel may be your last chance."

During the next two years, Daniel came often to Rice Produce Store on Perry Street. Charming as he was, when he kissed her, she felt nothing. "It was more exciting just looking at Matt," she told her friend Maggie in disappointment.

Then Daniel came with an engagement ring. "I have a wee gift for you." Opening up the box, he proudly reached for her hand. Limply, Annie let him put it on her finger. Staring down at her new ring, Annie debated with herself. *Sure, I don't have such feelings for him. But 'twould be nice to be engaged. I need to get married before I'm too old to have children. Maybe love will grow. Daniel loves me. What more do I need?*

Desperate as she was to get married, Annie accepted the ring. She loved seeing the surprise on her customers' faces as they noticed the ring. *Now they can't be calling me a spinster, no more no more.*

Uncle Edward and Aunt Katherine made an unexpected visit from Tyholland. She was glad she'd started a beef stew that morning, simmering on the stove in the apartment above the store. The kitchen smelled good when they went up for supper. Aunt Katherine helped Annie clear the table while Uncle Edward visited with Frank. Her hands in the dishwater, Aunt Katherine turned to Annie. "Annie, I have to tell you something. Uncle Edward heard rumors that Daniel likes the gambling, makes big bets on the horses. That's why he goes to Belfast so often. He's neglecting his little farm in Tyholland. When we heard about your engagement, we thought we should tell you. We know how angry you get with your brothers for gambling."

That was it. Annie decided to end it with Daniel. Her brothers were gamblers, she wasn't about to marry one. Daniel was shocked when Annie showed him her left hand without the ring. "Sure, and you forgot to tell me how you bet on the horses. I threw your ring away. Faith, you think I want to support you along with my brothers?"

Chapter 14

LETTERS IN THE MAIL

The postman delivered another letter with a postmark from America. The envelope lay on the counter, teasing Annie as she waited on Mrs. O'Neill. She had a difficult time acting patient as the elderly customer took her time choosing her produce. Before Mrs. O'Neill reached the door with her purchase, Annie snatched up the letter. One minute she wanted to tear it open, the next she was afraid to read it. She jammed the letter in her apron pocket.

Alone in her room that evening, she moaned as though in pain when she read, "I'm thinking of a visit back to Ireland."

Annie read the letter over and over, struggling with her conscience about the promise she made on her mother's deathbed.

She argued with herself, *Ma did not want me to have anything to do with Matt Donahue. But Ma is dead. My brothers depend on me to run this store. But they won't stop gambling. Why should I support them when they pay no attention to me? Sure, and they win tea sets and pretty dishes, but they don't put food on the table. James went off to New York and is happy with his new life.*

I know Ma begged me not to leave Ireland. But who is going to marry me? I've not met a man that I liked as well as Matt. I refused Daniel when he asked me to marry him. 'Twasn't difficult when I found out that Daniel loved to bet on the horses. He claimed he has the luck of the Irish and doesn't lose money, but winning streaks don't go on forever. He's kissed the blarney stone, that one.

I'm lonely . . . over twenty years I've been writing to Matt. "Tis time to marry. I want Matt so much. Oh, Matt, why don't you come back for me?

Annie agonized all night, struggling with her conscience. She said to herself, *Faith, and who else wants to marry you, Annie Rice? You want to run this store forever? You were sixteen when you met Matt. Now you're nearly forty. Should I write to Matt and ask him to come?*

Early in the morning, she grabbed paper and pen and wrote:

"Dear Matt:
Ma is dead. I'm sick of this store. I'm sick of my brothers thinking they can take anything they want without paying me. They keep eating up my profits and pay no attention to me.
If you come for a visit, you might have company on the way home."

Heart pounding, she rushed to the post office and shoved the letter into the slot before she changed her mind.

Two weeks later her best friend insisted on telling Annie her fortune. Maggie claimed she was fey but, scoffing at her friend's professed power to see into the future, Annie had resisted all previous efforts to speculate on her destiny. At this crucial time in her life, Annie decided it might not hurt to hear what Maggie would tell her.

Maggie predicted, "A short, dark-haired male is going to take a fair-haired lady out of this house and across water. I see them going up the aisle of a church carrying something. Then they're going across a large body of water, and it will be a turbulent journey."

Annie tossed and turned worrying about the letter she'd mailed to Matt. *What would he think? What did Maggie's prediction mean? Could she really see into the future? Was Matt coming for her? Would she marry him if he showed up?*

Chapter 15

A SURPRISE VISIT

Dungannon 1910

Annie was busy bagging Mrs. O'Connor's groceries while Mrs. O'Connor was gabbing a mile a minute. She heard the door open and glanced over out of the corner of her eye. A wave of dizziness hit her; she thought she was going to fall to the floor. Palms down on the counter, she tried to steady herself. *Breathe. It's not Matt. Breathe. It's just a man who looks like him. Breathe. It can't be Matt.*

Mrs. O'Connor asked, Are you all right, Annie? You look pale."

Concentrating on steadying herself, Annie jumped when the man touched her arm. "Annie."

Annie screamed, "Matt!"

Annie flung her arms around Matt, hoping she wouldn't crumple to the floor. Matt held her tightly. "I've come to ask you to marry me."

Annie did not hesitate. "Yes!"

Mrs. O'Connor stood wide-eyed watching the scene. "Is that the man from America you've been writing to, Annie?"

"Yes, yes! This is Matt from America! Matt, I can't believe it. It's really you! I just mailed you a letter two days ago. Did you get it already? No, of course not. You came!" Annie held her hand to her heart; it was pounding so fast her chest ached.

"I'm really here. Why don't you lock up the store, Annie, so we can talk?"

Reluctantly, Mrs. O'Connor left the store, but she told everyone she passed on the street, "Annie Rice's beau is here from America and asked her to marry him!"

They spent the day talking and making plans. Before going to bed, Annie took out the purple suit she'd carefully packed away in her trunk, hoping someday it would be her wedding dress. Burying her head in the purple wool, Annie wept with happiness.

In the morning, Maggie took care of the store while Annie took Matt to see Father Michael. Annie swore Maggie to secrecy before they left for the church, determined not to let her brothers know. "I'll not have them stopping me. You know how upset they'll be, Maggie."

Maggie nodded. "Who will tend the store for them if you leave?"

Annie tossed her head. "Sure, and do I care? Maybe they'll have to stop their gambling."

Father Michael listened to their story about their long correspondence.

"What do your brothers say?"

"I've not told them."

"Bans have to be posted for three weeks."

Matt said, "Father, I have to hurry back. An Indian friend is living on my homestead and taking care of my livestock, but winters in Minnesota are bitterly cold. 'Tis over two weeks already since I left home and 'twill be a long journey home—ten days to cross the ocean then a lengthy train ride to Minnesota."

Annie watched Father Michael struggle with his conscience. Frowning, the priest turned away. Walking to the front of the church, he kneeled down in front of the white marble altar and bowed his head. *Dear God, how can I ruin their happiness? What is the right thing to do?*

Holding hands, Annie and Matt stared at one another. Annie felt like she couldn't get enough air into her lungs as her thoughts whirled. *What if Father Michael won't marry us? Dear God, I can't lose Matt again.*

Father Michael stood beside them. "How can I refuse to marry you after the romantic story I just heard? Don't worry. I'll take care of the bans. You're wedding will take place on February third. I think God will understand our need for speed and forgive us for posting the bans in only three days instead of three weeks." Annie's glowing face was his reward.

Chapter 16

FINDING TIMMY

1910

Annie, 'tis is a favor I must ask. While you are busy with wedding preparations these three days, I need to go look for my brothers in Donaghmore. I cannot go back to America without checking on them."

Frowning, Annie stood thinking for a moment. Matt hoped she wouldn't be angry. Finally, she assured him, "I'd feel the same about my bothers, angry as I get at them. I'll tell my brother, Edward, to loan you a horse."

Riding through the country he'd walked so long ago, he thought about his father. *He was a good Da' until my mother died. Then he turned to drink. Sure, and he must have died of the drinking. But Timmy . . .* He prayed that Timmy was well. *I hated leaving him. How I wish he'd answered one of my letters.*

Riding up to the O'Brian estate, taking in the beautiful green landscape, he felt a pang of regret that he'd had to leave. Shaking his head, he reminded himself how much he had accomplished. *I'm a landowner, I have a successful farm, I have my freedom to do what I want, and I can vote.*

Bypassing the castle, which didn't look so huge after all his travels, he rode directly to the barn. Squinting to look at a man

71

working with the horses in a fenced area, he wasn't sure if his eyes were deceiving him. *Is that Da'? Cannot be Da'. Twenty years is a long time, especially with all his drinking.*

Studying the man from his horse, Matt waited while the man clambered the fence and started coming toward him. "Timmy!"

Stopping, his mouth open, the man stood frozen. After another searching look, he began running toward him. "Matt! Matt! "Tis really you?" Almost falling as he scrambled off the horse, Matt ran to him with open arms.

Sitting on hay bales, they couldn't talk fast enough as they learned about each other's life. Timmy told Matt that Da' had been killed by a horse. "He stopped drinking, though, Matt. He was doing pretty well, working with the horses. Our lives were much better. They brought Betty's Da', Granda' Daniel, in to help in the barn after you left. He had a special way with the horses, they really responded to him. Kelly said Granda' Daniel was too valuable to go back to shoveling manure. He took charge of the horses and I learned so much from him; after he died, I became manager of the estate, replacing Kelly.

"Come, you must meet Bridget, my wife. She'll want to feed you, too. And our two boys will want to meet you. One is named Matt, after you. The other is Daniel, after Granda'"

Bridget welcomed Matt warmly, saying, "I've heard about you forever, I have. Timmy worships you. And I've got a lovely Irish stew ready to dish up. Timmy, call the boys."

Timmy, Bridget, and the boys listened open-mouthed to Matt's tales of his journey to America, about his homestead in Minnesota, and about his upcoming marriage to Annie.

Staying overnight with them, Matt could see they were a happy family. His half-brothers were working on the estate, too, and in the morning, after enjoying the typical huge Irish breakfast that Bridget cooked, he went out to the barns to meet Terry and Michael. Matt invited all of them to the wedding, but they didn't think they could leave the horses. "We have a new group of Dartmoor horses to train before the polo matches begin again," they said.

One last time before leaving, Matt pleaded with Timmy to come to America. Shaking his head, Timmy said, "Bridget does not want to leave her family. We're happy here. Maybe someday we can come for a visit."

Slumping with disappointment, Matt barely noticed how slowly the horse was plodding along as they left the estate. His hope that Timmy would move to America dashed, he felt a pain in his heart. Suddenly, thoughts of Annie brightened his spirit; he straightened up in the saddle and slapped the reins for the horse to go faster. As the horse broke into a brisk trot, Matt patted his neck, saying, "Back to my sweetheart, Annie."

Matt did not notice the lack of sun on this soft day. The intermittent rain did not dampen his spirit, only his clothes; thinking about Annie kept him warm. *Tomorrow is my wedding day!*

Chapter 17

THE WEDDING

February 3, 1910

Her brother, Edward, was furious. "Ma will turn in her grave. Who will take care of the store? If James were here, he'd put a stop to this nonsense. You know how Ma felt." Annie's tears forced him to grudgingly give in to her wishes to marry Matt.

Frank sulked.

Sick with worry that her family would do something to stop the wedding, Annie prayed that nobody would interfere. Her oldest brother should have given her away, but because James had moved to New York, she asked Edward. "And don't you go disappearing to go gambling."

Maggie winked at Annie as she walked up the aisle on Edward's arm. Frank, looking grown-up in a new suit, sat in the front pew with a sad face. Annie's heart lurched and she almost stopped, but Matt smiled at her and held out his hand; she joined him at the altar. Her heart leaped as she saw how debonair he looked with his thick black hair, mustache, and handsome black suit.

Barbara helped Annie change clothes after the wedding ceremony. Her suitcases were packed and ready to go. It had been a tearful process, choosing what to take and what to leave behind. Fear clutched her stomach as she folded her wedding suit in layers of tissue paper. "What will my new life be like, living in a log cabin in the woods?"

Barbara said, "'Tis an exciting life you'll have!"

Kissing Frank goodbye brought a flood of tears. Annie felt like she was being torn in two. She turned a tear-stained face to Matt. "'Tis like saying goodbye to my own son. I've raised him all these years, since he was a wee toddler. Matt, can we send for him when we're settled in America?"

Edward said, "Annie, he's almost a man already."

Annie stamped her foot. "Fifteen is not a man. Besides, he'll have more opportunities in America. Matt, say he can come to live with us."

Impatient to leave and sad that Timmy refused to go to America, Matt promised.

Giving Frank one last hug, Annie declared, "We'll be sending for you, Frank. Matt said we could."

The newlyweds stayed overnight in Belfast, then caught the ferry to Scotland so Annie could say goodbye to her sister Minnie. Matt confessed, "On that misty morning in 1888, I almost turned back before getting on this ferry. I didn't want to leave you."

Minnie was overjoyed at seeing Annie. The sisters hugged each other and cried. She begged Annie to tell her news about Frank, the son she'd been forced to leave with her mother when she first came to Scotland. She'd only seen him a few times, but the empty place was still there in her heart, even though she'd had three daughters and a month ago had given birth to a boy. "My heart still longs for my first-born."

Taking advantage of their unexpected appearance, Minnie asked them to be godparents for her new baby. Coming back from making arrangements, she said, "I told the priest that my sister, the new bride, was here before sailing to America. Teddy will be baptized in the morning."

Annie carried Teddy into the church. Cuddling him, smelling his sweetness, an unexpected longing for her own baby washed over her. *Will I have children? I'm already thirty-eight.* She hugged Teddy tightly.

Standing at the baptismal font, Annie suddenly shivered. *Maggie's prediction! 'Tis true! We bumped heads and got married. Went across the Irish Sea to Scotland. Here I am, carrying Teddy down the aisle. Tomorrow we sail to America across the Atlantic Ocean. Will it be a turbulent journey?*

Straightening her back so she stood tall, she chided herself: *Faith, and what do I care? I have Matt.*

Section III
Irish Pioneers

Chapter 18

GOLDVILLE

1917

Sighing dreamily in the early morning quiet, Marie snuggled next to her little sister, Nellie. A second later, her eyes snapped open and butterflies whirled in her stomach. Bolting out of bed, she ran to the chair laid out with her new clothes.

After dressing carefully, Marie stood on tiptoe, peeking into the mirror to brush her short black hair. Satisfied, the six-year-old laid down the brush, then walked into the front room. Sitting carefully on the davenport, she reminded herself not to touch anything. The front room had to be kept nice for company.

Folding her hands in the lap of her new dress, trying not to fidget, she remembered how excited she'd been last year when she started kindergarten. She'd dressed herself every morning while Ma was out in the barn. Until that first cold morning in October when Ma insisted she had to wear long underwear. She'd struggled to pull her long brown stockings over the bulky underwear. When Ma came in from milking cows, Marie's bottom lip was quivering. "I hate this long underwear! I'm not wearing it!" She yanked off the ugly stockings and threw them on the floor.

Two-year-old Paddy was crying in his crib and Ma went in to get him. Plunking him on the floor beside Marie, Ma got down on her knees. Grabbing a stocking, she stretched it out, pushed it over Marie's foot, and jerked it up over the underwear. She grabbed the other one and put that on. "There! You will wear long stockings and underwear."

Marching into the indoor bathroom with the girls from her class and using a toilet that flushed was a special part of the day. Wearing her long underwear, she didn't dare use the bathroom. She was too worried that she wouldn't get the underwear and stockings tucked together again; they scratched at her all day.

After she went to bed that night she'd overheard her mother telling Pa, "'Tis too much trouble to get her ready. She can wait until next year when Nellie and Paddy will be older and she can dress herself." Sadness had seized her back then and it engulfed her again now as she thought about missing kindergarten the remainder of that year. Crying and moping around the house didn't work; Ma paid no attention. Of course, Nellie was happy to have her sister stay home. Well, now she was a year older and could dress herself completely.

The rising sun spread pink through the sky. A flash of light glinted from a quartz rock on the table near the window. A souvenir from the days he had worked in the gold mines at Rainy Lake City, Pa was very proud of it. "Not real gold. Fool's gold," Pa always corrected her when she called it gold. Matt Donahue, a short and wiry Irishman, emigrated from Ireland to find freedom and land. The Rainy Lake gold rush had helped him accomplish his dream.

Sliding off the davenport, Marie picked up the nugget, entranced by the gold flecks sparkling in the sun. Ma liked to tease her husband, "Your gold nugget is just another old rock." She'd say to Nellie and Marie, "Pa's a fool if he thinks his fool's gold is valuable. My china has more gold in it than that old rock." Dainty pink flowers and gold leaves were sprinkled over the off-white dishes. The golden leaves glittered when the sun poked its head through the window and sunbeams reached out to the china cupboard.

Whenever she used the china she told Marie and Nellie, "I wrapped each piece of precious china in my clothing and clean potato sacking. Not one dish broke on the long journey from Ireland to America."

Annie Donahue's favorites, though, were the Irish Belleek pieces she brought with her from Ireland as a new bride. Green shamrocks were painted on the pearly iridescent vase and miniature teapot that sat on the top shelf of the china cupboard, out of reach from curious fingers. Shamrocks brought good luck, but Marie knew it would be very bad luck to break the Belleek!

Pa teased, "We'll find gold on this land. The leprechauns have been hiding it from me, but we'll find it." Pa blamed leprechauns for any bad luck. "Leprechauns are little men dressed in green who create mischief. They only grow to three feet tall, but they're full of tricks," Pa explained.

Frustrated because she'd never gotten a glimpse of the little people who caused trouble, Marie pleaded, "I want to see a leprechaun!" After all, now she was a first grader and should know what they looked like.

"The little people hide from you. They won't let you see them."

Matt loved to tell about starting a new life in a new country in a new century. As often as she'd heard the story, Marie never tired of hearing it.

The day he discovered the rich soil on the banks of Rainy River, Matt squatted down to smell the earth, his pulse leaping with anticipation. He told Marie, "I tasted that dirt and it was so good I knew it was the land I'd been looking for. The air smelled of pine trees and birds were singing. 'Twas a sweet moment."

Marie always made a face at Pa. "You ate dirt!"

"Sure, and I did that. I was so excited, my heart pounded as hard as the hammer when I drove a stake in the ground for my claim. 'Twas the luck of the Irish that I filed the first claim for this land! The leprechauns weren't playing tricks on me that day!"

Marie glanced at the official document hanging on the wall. She didn't need to read to know that the U. S. Patent was dated November 28, 1900. Pa bragged about the date so often, she knew it by heart.

After he received the patent to the plats he'd marked, Matt worked at the mine until spring breakup, scrimping to save as much money as he could. "Snow still covered the ground when I set up a tent and began clearing my 160 acres. 'Twas cold, but I worked up a sweat."

As he labored, he marveled that he actually owned this land covered with towering trees. Every swing of the axe and every ache in his muscles had brought him closer to his dream. Each tall pine tree that crashed to the ground brought him one log closer to his cabin and more space for planting. Wiping his brow, hand at his aching back, he'd look around him and grin with satisfaction.

"Sure, and I would never own an inch of land or a single tree in Ireland, not at all," he repeatedly told his family. "Never would I own a horse, either. I'd be slaving for a rich landowner and we would be so poor you'd be thin as fence rails."

He'd chosen the name Goldville for his homestead. "Rainy Lake gold mines brought me here, but this rich Rainy River land kept me here."

Hearing the back door slam Marie snapped out of her trance, put down the fool's gold, and ran to the kitchen doorway.

Setting down two pails of milk, her mother said, "Up and dressed already? 'Tis barely breaking day."

For weeks, Marie had been asking: "When do I start school, Ma?"

Ma would say, "How many times have you asked me that? Go pester your Pa."

Out at the barn, she'd pet the horses, Kate and Pete. "Are Kate and Pete anxious for school, Pa?" Pa was the bus driver and the horses pulled the covered buckboard wagon that served as a school bus. In winter, Pa replaced the wagon with a sleigh.

Ma said, "Start cooking the bacon and eggs. If you're old enough to go to school, you're old enough to help." Marie flew to the wood stove before her mother lost her temper.

Bacon was sizzling in the black cast iron frying pan when Pa came whistling through the door. "I'm ready, Pa!" Marie ran to greet him.

"'Tis a vision. Can it be my little girl in that pretty dress? All ready to go to that new school, are ya? 'Tis a grand building with shiny marble floors and all."

Marie remembered the shiny floors and sitting by the fireplace while the kindergarten teacher read stories. She'd loved playing with the doll and doll buggy, but there would be no toys in first grade; she would be learning to read and count. She felt a pang as she thought about how much fun she'd missed because she couldn't finish kindergarten.

Marie scrambled into the school bus. Her face beaming, she waved to Ma, Nellie, and Paddy standing in the yard. Pa slapped the reins; Kate and Pete trotted down the two narrow paths leading to the dirt road to town.

At the first stop, the Hoey boys vaulted into the wagon, noisily fighting over seats while ignoring Marie. At the Thompsen house, Lorraine and her brother Roy clambered on. Lorraine Thompsen was only fifteen days older than Marie; Marie patted the space beside her. Lorraine sat down and they chattered and giggled the five miles to school.

Although Marie and Lorraine were friends, they seldom saw each other because both were busy with chores at home. Lorraine's straight black hair was neatly combed and her faded dress had been freshly laundered. Marie compared her pale skin to Lorraine's. Marie's skin burned and never turned tan, but Lorraine's was always brown. "'Tis Irish skin you have and Indian skin that Lorraine has. You both can be proud of your heritage," Ma told Marie whenever she complained.

On the muddy street by the newly completed school, Pa slapped the reins lightly. "Whoa, Kate. Whoa Pete. Here we are now." Butterflies began fluttering in her tummy as Marie looked at the grand brick building.

The boys hopped out of the wagon, but Pa came around to lift off the girls. Holding hands, Marie and Lorraine skipped into the school. A teacher stood in the hallway, smiling. "Are you in kindergarten?" she asked.

"No! First grade!" Marie and Lorraine answered in unison. They were big girls!

The teacher pointed where to go and Marie and Lorraine walked into a large room. "Look!" Marie pointed at small chairs and desks. "Won't it be fun to sit in them?" Remembering Ma's warning about always listening to the teacher, she didn't sit down until Teacher showed them their desks. Marie and Lorraine sat in the front row.

When all the children were settled, the teacher said, "My name is Miss Larson. Now, I want each of you to tell me your name and a little bit about yourself."

When it was Marie's turn she said, "I'm Marie and I live in Goldville. My Pa drives the school bus."

"Goldville?" Miss Larson asked. "Where is that?" Marie ducked her head, not sure how to give directions. When Marie didn't answer, the teacher asked: "Does the name Goldville have anything to do with the gold mines?"

Marie's face lit up. "My Pa worked in the gold mines. He has a big gold nugget."

Miss Larson said, "Your Pa worked in the gold mines! How interesting." She waited a moment, but Marie didn't know what else to add. She fidgeted until the teacher looked at Lorraine. "Tell us your name."

Nellie ran out the door when Marie got home from school. "I missed you, Marie!" she said forlornly and listened to every word about her big sister's first day at school.

After supper, Marie stared at Pa's nugget. Teacher seemed really interested in gold. When Pa came in from chores, she met him at the door. "Pa, tell me about when you worked at the gold mine."

Chapter 19

ROAD TO GOLD

A story about 1894

Marie hopped up on her father's lap and prompted, "Once upon a time . . ."

"Once upon a time I lived in the country of Ireland, a lush green island far, far away. I took care of horses for rich people who liked to play polo."

"And the rich people were named O'Brian and lived in a big castle."

"I had a dream of owning my own land and my own horses, so I sailed across a big ocean to America. I worked in a lot of places—New York, Pennsylvania, and Ohio. I worked in the coal mine in Tower City, Pennsylvania owned by a man who lived in Philadelphia. His name was Charlemagne Tower and he was so rich he bought two mountains and had two towns named after him. The second coal mine was in the Iron Range in Minnesota. It was called the Iron Range because it was on a great big mountain of iron ore. A settlement near the mines was named Tower in Mr. Tower's honor. They said he was a Civil War hero, too.

"A leprechaun whispered in my ear that people in Minnesota could get free land, so when I heard about that coal mine in Minnesota, I left Ohio. Sometimes I walked, sometimes I traveled by train, and I became employed at the Mesabi Mine owned by Mr. Tower.

"While I was working in Mr. Tower's coal mine, rumors started flying about a gold strike up north. Sure, and I didn't believe a word of it, not at all. Then newspapers began writing about the big gold rush to Rainy Lake City. Prospectors from far away were stampeding there to find gold. And here I was, only fifty miles away from it. My friend Mike McGuire and I got the idea we'd rather dig for gold ore instead of iron ore."

"You got gold fever!"

"Yup! But our fever got cooled down real quick. We nearly froze to death. We left in March so we could travel the Tower Ice Road. Going by land would have doubled the distance; it would have been 100 miles. The cold wind blew across that icy road something fierce. It whipped icy snow in our faces and we could hardly walk against it. But it was March and there had been some sunny days that had melted the ice; we had to watch carefully for thin ice. Sometimes we saw open water standing on the ice. At night howling wolves sounded close enough to pounce on us.

"Who was that man you walked with?"

"Boston O'Brien. He carried a gun, so we felt safer with him. But we found out later that he was an ornery outlaw who liked to terrorize people."

"Were you scared of him, Pa?

"No, we Irish stick together. He made sure none of the other scoundrels bothered me."

"Some men had funny names."

"Sure, and they did. Gold Bug Jimmy, Patty the Bird, Paddy the Keg, Curly Bedford, and One-Armed Sullivan were a few I remember."

"What happened to that one-armed man?"

"Well, the story I heard was that a young high school graduate from Minneapolis named Guy Parker was on his way to a teaching job in Koochiching. Parker hitched a ride with the mailman. They were traveling with a horse and sleigh over the Tower Route in the winter. One day it was 25 degrees below zero with snowdrifts on the ice. By the time they got to Rainy Lake City, the poor teacher was leading the exhausted horse. Imagine how disappointed the teacher must have been when Rainy Lake City turned out to be a ghost town.

"The teacher walked into Lake Shore House, the only hotel left on the island. One-Armed Sullivan was lying on the floor by the door with his Indian wife on the floor moaning over him. The dead man was still bleeding from a gunshot wound from an old enemy, William O. Randolph, who had just settled a long feud. Men were drinking at the bar as though nobody had just been murdered. They told the shocked Parker, "He was nothing but a 'no-good-for-nothing bum.'"

"Matt!" Engrossed in Pa's story, Marie jumped as Ma yelled from the bedroom where she was putting Paddy to bed. Hastily coming out of the bedroom, she stood with hands on hips. "Would that be a bedtime story for a wee girl? You'll be giving her bad dreams."

Pa winked at Marie. "'Tis true!"

"I won't have nightmares, Ma. I promise!"

Ma flounced back into the bedroom.

"'Tis nothing to be afraid of. That incident happened in 1901. A few years earlier, when I arrived at Rainy Lake City, it was an island in the wilderness plunked in the middle of a huge lake. It was a tent city and most of the tents were saloons. Just like the Wild West, there were gunslingers with trigger-happy fingers. But everybody worked hard to hack out that gold frozen in sold quartz rock."

"There were Indians, too."

"Yes, but they weren't wild. They were nice people."

"You had an Indian friend, didn't you, Pa."

"Sure, and I did. 'Tis a long, long name—Way-We-Zhe-Quam-Aish-Kung. At the gold mine, they nicknamed him King. King took me fishing a few times and then came out to the homestead to take care of my animals when I went back to Ireland to marry your mother. The gold mines had all been closed by then."

"You didn't care when the mines went broke."

"Nope. I had 160 acres of land staked out. I named it Goldville because that black dirt was my gold! Look outside. All that land out there is ours. But someday the good leprechauns might help us find that pot of gold!"

Marie was pretty sure Pa was only joking about the gold and leprechauns. But she said, "A good leprechaun already helped, Pa. Because he brought you to the gold mines!"

"Sure, and you're right! And we always have food. When I was your age, many nights I went to bed with an empty stomach growling."

"And our streets are paved in gold!"

"Well, we heard the rumor that the streets of Koochiching were paved in gold. The town was named Koochiching in 1894 when I arrived at Rainy Lake City, but it was changed to International Falls in 1904." Marie was glad the town's name had been changed because her tongue stumbled over the Indian name, Koochiching.

"Off to bed with ya now. 'Tis school again tomorrow."

Chapter 20

CHRISTMAS DOLLS

1918

"If you kids don't calm, down there will be no Santa stopping here tonight!" Annie stopped plucking feathers on the goose she was preparing for Christmas dinner. She took special pride in her Christmas dinner. Busy cooking and baking, she became angry with Marie, Nellie, and Paddy as they ran squealing through the house.

Ma always got a little crabby when company was coming. The Holts and Mr. and Mrs. Joe Baker were coming to Christmas dinner. Mr. Baker's uncle might be coming too. Alexander Baker School was named after him and Marie had heard him called the "founder of International Falls." Mr. Baker looked a little scary to her with his long white hair and deep set eyes. With his long white beard, he would have looked like Santa Claus if he'd smiled a little and acted jolly instead of gloomy.

Pa had told her the story about the Baker family. "They were pioneers when hardly anybody else lived in the settlement; they came from Scotland. Although Mr. Baker was born in Scotland, he fought in the Civil War soon after he arrived in America. Lots of Irishmen fought in the Civil War. After the Civil War was over, he squatted on the banks of Rainy River overlooking Koochiching Falls. In 1900 Mr.

E. W. Backus and Mr. W. F. Brooks came looking for property for their future mill and purchased most of Baker's land."

Marie's thoughts were interrupted when Pa banged through the door with an armful of firewood. "Matt, I can't be fixing dinner for company tomorrow with these wild ones driving me crazy. I have to pluck the feathers off the goose and the chickens for tomorrow's dinner and there's more baking to do. I still have to fix that oyster stew that you insist on having every Christmas Eve. How do you expect me to do it all with this fighting and yelling going on?"

"You kids get dressed and come out to the barn," Pa ordered. "There's lots of work out there to keep you out of mischief. Marie, help Paddy into his snowsuit." Obligingly, Marie struggled to help Paddy into his winter gear.

Wrapping a muffler around her neck, Nellie asked, "Should we check the chickens for eggs, Pa?" Nellie loved animals, even chickens. After being chased by a goose once, Marie wasn't as crazy about them as Nellie.

"Sure, and 'twould be a help, Nellie. No scrambled eggs today, mind," he cautioned Paddy who clenched them so tightly they broke in his hands.

Their faces rosy from the cold when they came back in, Paddy and Nellie kicked off their boots and scattered their mittens, scarves, and snowsuits helter-skelter. Automatically, Marie picked them up and hung them neatly on the pegs by the back door. It was her responsibility to help Ma with the younger ones. Sadness swallowed her briefly as she thought about missing kindergarten because she'd had to help Ma last year. But Christmas wasn't the time for gloom. Today was the time for joy and presents.

Marie knew Ma was in a better mood when she gave her a smile and said, "Why don't you hang up your stockings for Santa Claus?" Nellie and Paddy whooped with excitement. "Get stockings out of your drawers."

Marie rummaged in her drawer for brown stockings without holes. She hated wearing those stockings, but tomorrow morning there would be an apple or orange, candy, and nuts inside. By the time they finished hanging the stockings, Pa came stomping in from the barn and it was time to set the table for supper.

They went to bed without a struggle, but Marie and Nellie whispered until Ma yelled at them to get to sleep. Nellie fell asleep right away, but Marie lay awake, listening. Ma and Pa were murmuring and walking around. Curiously, she stretched her neck to see into the front room. Ma had just set something under the tree. Leaning further out of bed to see what it was, she drew in her breath. A doll! A doll dressed in blue. Marie's heart sank. Anything blue went to Nellie.

But what was Pa putting under the tree? It was a doll with a pink dress! Shivering with excitement, Marie squeezed her eyes shut and willed herself to sleep so morning would get there fast.

It was still dark when she bounced out of bed. "Nellie, wake up! It's Christmas!"

Racing to the Christmas tree, Marie bent down to pick up the pink doll. Nellie, sleepily following her sister, stopped short when Marie burst into tears.

"What's wrong?" Nellie looked at the doll Marie held, then leapt back in horror and screamed.

Ma and Pa came running out of their bedroom. "What's going on?"

"Marie's doll is blind!"

There were two open holes where the doll's eyes should be.

"It's horrid. Ugly." Lower lip trembling, Marie threw the doll down and stomped back to her bedroom. She flung herself down on the bed, kicking and wailing.

"Marie, get back here," Ma yelled. Marie continued her forlorn wailing.

Pa came in and sat on the bed, putting his arm around Marie. "'Tis a shame, indeed. The doll got injured on its way here, riding in the train. It must have gotten hot because the eyes melted and fell out. Sure, and it came all the way from New York. A man came into Uncle Jim's saloon in the Bronx selling dolls and he was buying one for his little girl, Molly. 'Twas nice of him to remember you, and Nellie, too."

Marie automatically began to nod, then violently shook her head. "I don't care. I hate it!"

Pa patted Marie's shoulder. "Tell you what. I'll see what I can do to get the eyes back in."

"Oh, Pa. Can you fix it?" Marie wiped her eyes and followed Pa back to the front room.

When breakfast was over, Pa started working on the doll. Gently pulling the hair back from the doll's forehead he cut a slit in the top of the head and fished with his finger for the eyes. The eyes kept slipping away, but finally he pulled them out one at a time. Ma glued the eyes back into the hole, and then glued the hair back over the slit. She handed it to Marie. "There. Good as new!"

Marie and Nellie stared at the doll. The doll's eyes stared back. Marie laid it down, but its eyes stayed wide open, staring at them.

When Nellie laid her doll down, the eyes closed. She picked it up and they popped open. As though worried Marie would snatch it away, Nellie put her doll against her shoulder and held it tightly.

Marie carried her doll into the front room to the rocking chair. Rocking and hugging her doll, Marie whispered, "Don't worry, I still love you." Tenderly smoothing the doll's pink dress, Marie fought down jealousy.

The two sisters played with their dolls the rest of the day, but Marie had an ache in her heart that would not go away.

Next morning, Ma put both dolls on top of the piano. "They're too nice to play with. You can look at them from here. See how good they look up there on the piano?"

The piano was new. Marie had been begging for piano lessons since school started because the girls in town bragged about taking lessons from Miss Lynch. A few of Ma's friends had daughters taking lessons too, and Miss Lynch was choir director at church, a good Catholic lady. Ma convinced Pa that the girls needed a piano. They'd gotten the piano in early December and Marie had already had two lessons with Miss Lynch.

After Christmas, whenever Marie practiced her scales, the dolls silently watched and listened. Marie would glance up to see whether they liked the song; sometimes she thought she saw her doll smile.

Chapter 21

TENTH ANNIVERSARY
February 3, 1920

"Happy Anniversary, Annie! Ten years already." Pa's voice drifted into Marie's sleep.

"Sure, and didn't we waste a lot of years! Twenty-two years it took you to come back for me! We could have grandchildren by now!"

"Well, at least all three kids are in school now. That makes it easier for you."

"Sure, and having three babies in three years was not easy, I can tell you that, Matt Donahue."

At school later that day, Marie thought about her parents. She loved hearing the story about how they met when Pa was on his way to America. She knew that was why her mother and father were older her friends' parents—because they'd waited so long to get married.

Would Ma be trying on her wedding dress today? Proud that she still fit into the purple suit she'd worn on her wedding day, Ma would look in the mirror, turning from side to side, smoothing the skirt over her hips. Although she had a generous bosom, her hips stayed slim. Modeling the wedding suit for her family was the only time Ma showed any vanity.

But Marie worried because last year Ma had locked herself in the bedroom, moaning with pangs of homesickness for Ireland. "Sure, and 'tis a long time since I left Ireland. Will I ever get back? Will I see my family again, Matt Donahue?" Marie hated it when Ma got in one of her black Irish moods.

While Marie and Nellie were washing supper dishes, Annie went into the bedroom to take her wedding dress wrapped in tissue out of the trunk. A screech like an animal caught in a trap startled them. Nellie flung her dishtowel down and Marie grabbed it to wipe her hands as they dashed into the bedroom. Annie screamed, "Moths! Look at these holes! Moths ate holes in my dress."

Grabbing her coat, Marie ran to the barn. "Pa, Pa, come quick!" Pa came running out the barn door. "What's wrong?"

"Moths. Holes in Ma's wedding dress," Marie panted.

"Holes?" Pa looked perplexed, but he ran with Marie. Annie sat at the kitchen table, head down in her arms, bawling. Marie tiptoed over to the stove and put on the kettle for tea.

Chapter 22

Who took Kate?

January 1922

"Pa's here with the school bus," Ma said as they heard the horses stomping outside. She cautioned her daughters, "The thermometer reads twenty-five degrees below zero, so dress warm."

Marie had one arm in the sleeve of her warm winter coat when Pa burst through the door. His face was crimson and his body stiff with anger. "Kate's all sweaty. She's been ridden. Somebody stole my horse out of the barn last night. 'Tis a sorry man he'll be if I catch him."

Ma angrily turned from the stove. "'Tis a bad thing when a man's horse gets stolen."

"At least Kate is back," Marie said.

"'Tis true, Matt. Whoever took Kate brought her back safe and sound. You can be thankful for that," Ma said.

"I still don't like it at all, not at all. But time is wasting. Load up the sled with the milk and foot warmers. We have to be off." Pa banged out the door.

Annie went to the wood stove where charcoal slabs were heating on top of the coals. They were red hot and she carefully used tongs to put them into trays that pulled out of the foot warmers. After Marie and Nellie finished dressing, Ma tucked them into the sled with a warm blanket and the foot warmers.

The tug-of-war to pull overshoes over her shoes wore her out, but Marie felt lucky that she had them. Lorraine and her brother didn't have overshoes and their Pa wouldn't let them use the foot warmers because he said they would ruin their shoes. Sometimes Lorraine took off her shoes to warm her feet in her hands.

As the kids piled on the sled, Marie and Nellie told them about Kate. "Who'd steal a man's horse?" the oldest Hoey boy asked. The neighbor boys knew that Kate and Pete played an invaluable part in Matt's rigid routine each day.

Jabbering fast and furiously about the mystery, the trip to school went quickly and nobody noticed the cold. On subzero days, they were usually shivering by the time they reached school, but today when Matt stopped the horses, the oldest Hoey boy said, "We got here quick as a jack rabbit today!"

Chapter 23

SOLVING THE MYSTERY

1922

Pa went to the phone and cranked the handle. He'd made lots of inquiries in town the day before but had come up with no clues on who had taken Kate. Ma convinced him to call the sheriff.

"Amanda, is that you? How are things going? That was a terrible thing, terrible." Amanda's husband, policeman Wilbert McMicken, had been shot in 1922 when he trapped two men inside a shack and they blasted bullets through the door, hitting both patrolman McMicken and County Sheriff Hughes Van Etten. The criminal they had pursued had stolen some checks at the Markowitz store and Burton Department Store, but now both the thief and his friend were guilty of murder. A large posse killed the friend, and the thief was convicted and imprisoned.

Marie remembered what an uproar that had stirred. Shaking his head, Pa had said, "If the man had just turned himself in, two good men wouldn't have lost their lives and left behind widows and orphans. Just over a little bit of money." A year after the shooting, Amanda, began working at International Telephone Company to support her five children.

"Amanda, can you get me Sheriff Reidy? No, not an emergency, just want to talk to him."

"Sheriff Reidy? Matt Donahue here. I want to report a stolen horse . . . It happened last night . . . Yeah . . . Well, somebody must have brought her back and left her all sweaty in the barn. Be lucky poor old Kate doesn't get sick and die on me . . . No kidding . . . How he is now . . . I'll come to the jail . . ."

Matt turned to his family standing with questioning faces. "Sheriff picked up my old friend Mike McGuire early this morning. He was wandering the streets in bad shape. I'm going to the jail and talk with old Mike."

"Do you think he stole Kate?" Paddy asked.

"Don't know."

Marie said, "When I went to the well to get milk for Ma, the syrup can was empty." There was always a syrup pail of milk hanging from a rope in the well to keep it cool and Ma made sure it was kept filled. "It had lots of milk in it yesterday. Whoever took Kate must have gotten the milk too."

"Jail's a good place for that man if he took your horse. Don't go getting soft on him and dragging him back here to sober him up." Annie didn't appreciate some of the people Matt befriended.

"Don't you worry. I'll not be helping anybody who treated Kate badly."

They peppered questions at Matt before he could get his jacket and hat off when he returned from the jail. "Yes, it was poor old Mike. He started out walking to Littlefork but got tired and decided to borrow my horse. Said the house was dark or he'd have asked me first, but knowing I'd have let him use it, he up and took it. Got drunk with the friend he was visiting and didn't have the sense to take care of Kate when he rode back from Littlefork and put her in the barn. How he got to town the sheriff and I will never know. Apparently he was still staggering around because Sheriff saw him and threw him in jail."

"Is he still in jail?" Annie asked.

"Yup."

Marie asked, "Did you ask him if he drank our milk?"

"That he did. Said he had a powerful thirst when he brought Kate back and went to the well for water. He saw the syrup can with milk hanging there and drank that instead."

"How could he see at night?"

"'Twas a full moon."

Ma told Marie, "Go get the pail and bring it in so I can wash it."

The rest of that Saturday they all were busy with their chores. Ma enjoyed inviting friends over for Sunday dinner, which meant Saturdays were filled with baking, cooking, and cleaning. Several families were frequent guests: Dr. and Agatha Withrow, Benny and Jenny Baker, Walt and Peggy Holt, Bob and Ann Irvin. Annie enjoyed the compliments on her cooking.

A few weeks after Kate had been stolen, Dr. and Mrs. Withrow stopped by while out riding in their car. Marie and Nellie were hauling water from the well when they drove up. The pails were too full and water was sloshing out over their legs. Dr. Withrow jumped out of the car and took a pail from each of them. "You shouldn't fill these pails so full, little ladies. They're too heavy for you and you lose most of it anyway."

Nellie said, "We don't like making so many trips to the well."

Marie knew Dr. Withrow thought a lot of Pa and Pa thought a lot of him. Pa was always saying that Doc treated people whether they could pay or not. "'Tis few people who pay in cash. He gets paid in potatoes or other crops."

Dr. Withrow was one of Marie's favorite people, not only because he respected Pa, but because he treated her like an adult. One day he'd told Marie, "Your Pa and I have been good friends for many years, long before he married your Ma. I'd stop to visit him a few minutes whenever I walked the twenty miles to Littlefork to see a patient. Your Pa always gave me a nice cold glass of milk out of the well. Milk never tasted so good anywhere else. If Matt wasn't around, I'd just help myself. Matt didn't want me to go home thirsty."

"Mmmm." Dr. Withrow sniffed the aroma as he entered the kitchen with the pails of water. While pouring it into the stove reservoir, he peeked into the simmering pot. "Is that your delicious chicken and dumplings I smell?"

Phyllis Karsnia

"It certainly is. Can you stay for supper?" Annie asked.

"My mouth is watering already. You make the best chicken and the fluffiest dumplings in the whole county!"

Dr. Withrow tromped off to the barn to find Matt. Mrs. Withrow settled into a chair to keep Annie company in the kitchen. Watching Marie set the table, Mrs. Withrow said, "Marie, you are such a help to your mother. She's lucky to have a helpful girl like you."

Marie looked up in surprise when her mother answered, "Faith, and she is. I don't know how I could manage without her." Ma seldom gave compliments and it made Marie feel warm and tingly inside.

"Katherine's a big help to me, too. My three preferred staying at home today instead of coming for a ride with us. Tom's old enough to take on the responsibility of watching his young brother." Agatha Withrow's daughter, Katherine, was the middle child sandwiched between two boys, Tom and Joe. Tom and Katherine were a few years older than Marie, so she didn't know them very well.

Ma was dishing up the chicken when Pa said, "Sure, and something strange happened here about a month ago. I went out to the barn and poor old Kate was all tired and sweaty. Somebody rode her and then brought her back."

Dr. Withrow struck the table with his fist. "By gosh, Matt. I hope we don't have a horse thief on the loose."

"No. It was my old friend, Mike McGuire. The drink is getting to him something awful. Sheriff had him in jail. I was fighting mad when I saw her all sweaty and not rubbed down."

Nellie made everybody laugh when she said, "I told Pa maybe the leprechauns had taken her."

Mrs. Withrow, as Irish as the Donahues, observed, "Leprechauns can always be blamed when bad things happen!"

Chapter 24

LIFE ON THE FARM
1922

Matt took great pride in Annie's accomplishments as a good cook. After the poverty he'd suffered in Ireland, he felt immense satisfaction at being able to provide so well for his family. He had one of the best farms in Koochiching County, working diligently day after day. With Annie's help, his farm and his delivery business flourished. Neither of them was afraid of hard work.

Each morning, after dropping the children at school, he delivered eggs and milk to his customers in town. Without wasting time in town, Matt and the horses returned home so Matt could cut firewood. He sold lots of firewood, but his two biggest customers were St. Thomas Church and Koochiching County Courthouse. Their big furnaces gobbled up wood on cold days. Marie, amazed that her father had so much strength for such a small man, liked watching him cut down the trees when she was home. He would throw the logs on the wagon as though they weighed hardly more than a feather. After the wagon was full, he harnessed up the horses and hauled the wood to town to sell for $4.00 a cord.

The horses were always given a much-deserved rest before setting out on a second trip to town to deliver the firewood. Matt treated his horses well, not only because they were worth their weight in gold, but because he thought of them as friends. Ever since he'd been a wee lad taking care of the horses and sheep on the O'Brian estate in Ireland, he'd had a special kinship with animals.

Every afternoon after dropping off his second load of milk or firewood, Pa picked up the students for their return trip home. Marie was tickled that her Pa was the bus driver. It gave her a chance to tell him about her day and he often told her little stories about his customers.

On Sundays, her family attended St. Thomas Aquinas Church, just across the street from her school. Sitting in the pew, the sun streaming through the stained glass windows, Marie basked in the amber light that gave the church a heavenly glow. Not understanding the Latin words, she'd gaze around proudly at the church Pa had helped build.

Pa was one of the first people in the Catholic parish. He had helped build the first church, too—Church of the Holy Apostles. She'd heard him telling about those early days. "There were only fifty members when we made the decision to build a church. The priests in Fort Frances helped us out—we didn't have a priest yet. They approved of our big undertaking. People had to take a ferry across to Fort Frances to worship before Church of the Holy Apostles was built. The bridge over to Fort Frances hadn't been built yet, and it took a lot of effort to go over for a church service on Sunday morning. Some people couldn't even afford the ferry fees." Marie barely remembered going to that church, but she thought the name sounded holy.

Pa and Dr. Withrow had talked about how Mr. E. W. Backus had developed the Rainy River country with all his business ventures. "Backus brought in lots of people to work here, either at his lumber company, the paper mill, or on the dam construction. We had to build another new church because that first white frame structure became too small in just a few years. In April 1913, the Catholic congregation confidently decided to construct a 'magnificent and spacious church.'"

The dam was being excavated by Koochiching Falls on Rainy River. Mr. Backus, a director and co-owner of Minnesota and

Ontario Paper Company (usually shortened to Mando or M&O), wanted to harness the turbulent falls to power his pulp and paper mill. The church members were jubilant when the rock blasted at the dam site was offered to the Catholic Church. Matt volunteered to haul the rock from the International Dam to the church site and the blue granite soon started to form the walls of St. Thomas Church. Unfortunately, the unexpected $700.00 bill following the "free" rock blasted a hole in the building budget, setting off some short fuses among the contributors.

Annie was very angry about the bill. Busy with babies, she did not appreciate Matt's absences from home to haul the rock to begin with. Marie overheard the story many times as Annie complained to her friends over tea, "Marie was only two years old when Matt started hauling rock in 1913. That was the year Nellie was born. When Paddy was born a year later, Matt was still hauling rock, leaving me alone with three babies. After Matt donated many hours to hauling rock, the church had to raise more money to pay for it! Paddy had to be baptized in the basement because the upstairs of the church wasn't finished until 1916."

Marie wondered how Pa had managed to do all his work on the farm when he was hauling rock. Now, the whole family shared in the busy daily routine. Every morning while it was still pitch black, Marie was awakened by Pa stirring up the ashes and chucking firewood into the stove before he went out to the barn to milk.

Making breakfast had been Marie's job since that first day of first grade. In the winter she shivered while waiting for the stove to get hot enough to heat up the frying pan. The house was freezing cold because Annie was so scared of fire, she wouldn't let any wood be put into the stove before going to bed. Wind and cold air blew through the log walls, frosting them up no matter how much Pa plugged them with old clothes and rags. She dreaded the days when blizzards blew so fiercely that the house never warmed up and snowdrifts piled up so high Pa had to push hard to open the door.

Paddy didn't have any chores yet because he suffered from Rheumatic Fever, but Nellie's job was to carry the pails of milk from the barn into the milk shed. Ma washed the milk bottles at night and then carried them to the milk shed in the morning. Marie began frying the eggs when Ma came in for the bottles.

In the milk shed, Annie filled the tall bottles with the fresh milk, then placed the bottled milk into a pan with cold water and ice. The milk couldn't be topped with the round cardboard caps while it was still warm from the cow. While the milk cooled, Annie ate breakfast with the family.

With the well and a storage space for ice both located in the shed, it was an ideal place for bottling the milk. Ice didn't melt in winter, but in summer an icehouse with sawdust prevented it from melting too quickly. When the ice chunks that Pa cut from the river in the winter were all gone, Pa called the iceman.

Mr. Turenne was a popular man when he delivered the ice. Marie, Nellie, and Paddy would crowd around the back of his truck, watching as he picked up a huge cold square of ice with large tongs, slinging it over his shoulder and carrying it into the shed. On hot summer days, ice dripped down his leather apron. When he came back out of the shed, Mr. Turenne usually took pity on the three faces waiting hopefully. He'd scoop up slivers of ice chipped from the large cakes of ice and hand them out like candy. Ice chips (after picking out the sawdust) quenched thirst like nothing else and were savored as thoroughly as an ice cream cone.

After breakfast, Annie hurried out to cap the milk, getting it ready for Matt's morning delivery. There were times when customers didn't pay for the milk. No matter how much Annie fussed about unpaid bills, Matt insisted, "Sure, and the babies need the milk, now don't they? If they can't afford to pay eight cents for a quart of milk, do you think I can take it away from them? 'Tis little enough it costs me to keep the babies from starving."

A reservoir in the cook stove kept water warm for washing faces and dishes. And a teakettle was always bubbling on the stove for making tea and scalding dishes before they were dried. Carrying pails of water from the well was an endless job, but the girls were thankful that they didn't have to carry water for washing clothes. Pa said Savard's Laundry saved him money. "We could hardly buy soap for the dollar it costs at Savard's each week," he said.

Ma agreed. "Sure, and 'tis the hard water that ruins them."

Savard's Laundry offered free delivery service, picking up and delivering laundry with a horse and cart. Because Pa delivered milk to customers living on Second Street next door to the laundry, he dropped off their dirty clothes himself. When he picked up the clothes at the end of the day, they had been washed, dried in big tumbler dryers, and neatly folded. As Ma heated the black flatiron on the stove she liked to remark, "'Tis a fine job they do at Savard's Laundry. The dryers leave the clothes with fewer wrinkles, making my job of ironing much easier."

Chapter 25

A LATE SPRING

1923

St. Patrick's Day blew in with March's third snowstorm. Would winter never end? Spring seemed a long way away.

In spite of the weather, the Donahue family was looking forward to the special Irish holiday. Pa always brought treats on St. Patrick's Day and Ma cooked a traditional Irish supper of corned beef and cabbage. Marie's mouth watered with anticipation for the special meal bubbling on the stove.

Ma needed cheering up after the hard winter. Ireland rarely had snow and Annie did not appreciate Minnesota blizzards. Marie and Nellie hoped that the Irish holiday would pull her out of the black mood. Pa was smiling when he walked into the house with his hand behind his back. "Sure, and the leprechauns left a package outside."

Nellie and Paddy rushed at Pa. Feeling that twelve was too old to act childish, Marie hung back. Pa gave them each a bag of candy, and then handed a small round package to Annie.

"A new record? *I'll Take You Home Again Kathleen*. My favorite song! Besides *Irish Eyes are Smiling*. Oh, Matt!" It reminded Marie of how excited they'd all been when Pa bought the phonograph at Charlie Wirt's store. They'd spent many evenings listening to songs. It would be nice to have a new record. Annie walked over to put the cylindrical record into the sleeve of the Edison phonograph. Cranking it up, she stood listening with her head cocked. Marie felt her heart sink when Ma's face crumbled and tears rolled down her cheeks. Pa looked bewildered. "Why are you crying?"

"Sure, and I'm lonesome! I miss my sister Minnie something fierce! I even miss my brothers! They gambled away their money, but I miss them. I want to go back to Ireland!" Annie put her head on Matt's shoulder and sobbed.

He patted her clumsily. "Some day, Annie. Some day you will go back."

By April Fool's day, the snow was finally dwindling away. Although it was a bleak and dreary morning, it was warm and cozy in the kitchen with wood crackling in the stove and the smell of fresh bread baking. Ma told Marie and Nellie, "When the bread is cooled enough, you can take a loaf to Mr. Regan."

Wintry winds nipped at their legs as Marie and Nellie walked the half-mile to the old bachelor's house. Marie liked going to see their soft-spoken neighbor. He was built small like Pa and talked with a clipped accent that sounded much more formal than her parents' Irish brogue. But, even though Pa told how the Irish and the English had been fighting in Ireland for centuries, Pa and Henry Regan got along fine. Mr. Regan willingly pitched in when Pa needed help on the farm.

Mr. Regan had helped his next-door neighbor, Jerry McGowen, build his cabin. Mr. McGowen, a brawny Irishman with bristly red whiskers, intimidated all the kids in the neighborhood. The boys griped about "mean old McGowen." Lorraine told Marie that her brothers weren't ever allowed on his property, and Marie had heard him cussing when she walked past his place.

Mr. Regan greeted them at the door. "It's nice to see you two rays of sunshine on such a gray day. C'mon in out of the cold wind."

"We've brought you a loaf of Ma's bread fresh out of the oven."

"Come in and sit down with me and we'll have a slice of that good bread right now." Mr. Regan got out a knife and sliced the bread. "And would you look at this?" He reached into the cupboard. "I have some of your Ma's strawberry jam to spread on it."

Marie had been admiring the stack of neat kindling by the wood stove. "Mr. Regan, how do you cut your kindling so evenly?"

"I enjoy whittling away at it. Gives me something to do on a cold winter night."

Marie said boldly, "Those sticks look like they'd make good kites."

"They would. Would you like some sticks? That wind should make this a good day for flying kites." Mr. Regan bent down to gather a handful from his wood box.

"That's plenty. Thank you, Mr. Regan."

"These might not be long enough. I'll cut some longer pieces for you. Walking to a big toolbox in the corner of his kitchen, he opened up the curved lid and chose a small planer from the tools neatly organized inside the box.

Grabbing his plaid jacket, Mr. Regan went outside with them. He chopped neat slices of kindling with his axe, then planed them until they were perfect for kites. "Don't want you to get any splinters." The sisters waved good-bye as they left his driveway.

When they got home, Ma found her prettiest scraps of cloth for the tails while Marie made paste out of flour and water. Marie and Nellie were at the kitchen table folding newspapers for their kites when Pa yelled through the door, "Come see the moose!"

The girls threw down their unfinished kites and ran after Pa. "Where, Pa, where?"

"Up on the hill. Hurry up before he gets away."

"I can't see it!"

"Up there." Pa pointed to the top of the hill.

Panting by the time they stopped, they looked in every direction. "Where is it?"

"April Fool!"

Ma and Pa were laughing when Marie and Nellie went back inside. Pa said, "Sure, and the leprechauns chased the moose away before you got there."

Glaring at her parents, Marie plunked down to finish working on her kite. 'Twasn't funny, she thought as she finished pasting her kite together. Holding it gingerly, she went outside and began running in the field. No matter how fast she ran, it only flew up a short ways, then crashed down, getting tangled in the fence. Frustrated, she decided to give it one last try and ran as fast as she could. She stumbled and fell to the ground. "Ooowwww! My foot!"

Blood oozed from her shoe. I'll bleed to death, she thought wildly. How did I get cut? She saw the long curved blade of a scythe beside her foot, rusty from lying in the field all winter. The tip of the blade sticking up through dead brown weeds had cut through her shoe and gashed her foot.

Walking on the heel of the injured foot, she limped as fast she could, screaming "Ma, Ma!" At the barn harnessing Kate and Pete, Matt heard the screaming and ran to his daughter. Pulling off her shoe and seeing the blood spurting from her foot, he scooped her up in his arms and ran with her to the house.

"Get bandages," he yelled as Annie came running out of the house.

Annie put clean cloths over the gash and pressed down hard on the wound. When the bleeding let up, she washed and bandaged the deep cut. Grabbing the teakettle, she soaked bread in hot water, then added a few drops of Lysol. "Lie down so I can put this bread poultice on your foot. We don't want it to get infected."

Marie refused supper. "I'm sick to my stomach and my foot hurts." She felt sorry for herself as she lay on the bed with her foot throbbing. After supper, Annie fixed another bread poultice. The foot treated, she took Marie's doll off the piano and gave it her.

"I'm too old to play with dolls, Ma."

"Hold it anyway, Marie. Your Uncle Jim sent it to you from New York, remember? She can lie here and keep you company."

After Ma left the room, Marie cuddled with the doll. It did take her mind off the pain for a while. "I took care of you after your surgery on your eyes. Now you're taking care of me," she whispered to the doll.

Marie enjoyed the doll's company until she was able to get up. She limped around for several days until the gash in the foot was healed. However, a month later she complained to her mother, "Look, Ma, I can't move my big toe at all!"

Annie stopped kneading the bread to look down at Marie's foot. "Sure, and what do you need that toe for anyway?"

Every morning when she got out of bed, Marie wiggled her toes, hoping the big toe would move. Many months later, she noticed that her toes all wiggled back at her. It was her secret Christmas present.

Chapter 26

DISCUSSIONS ON THE RIVERBANK
June 1924

Rainy River sparkled in the June sunshine as Marie and Nellie sat on the riverbank during a rare break from chores. Soon they'd have to help Ma with lunch because Mr. Abbott, the county agent, and another man were testing the cattle for tuberculosis. At the supper table last night Pa had told them, "County Agent Abbott has arranged for all of us stockholders in the Dairymen's Association to have our cattle tested and he's trying to get the other farmers to test, too. He secured Dr. Denison from Bemidji to test the cattle for fifty cents a head. I heard that some of the cows he's already tested have had a reaction. Agent Abbott and the doctor will both be here tomorrow. I hope we can get all thirty-three done in one day. I'm not sure how long it will take."

Matt was proud that he'd become a shareholder in the Dairymen's Association, the first International Falls creamery, in 1923. Annie appreciated the fact that she no longer had to wash 150 to 200 milk bottles every day because the milk was delivered to the creamery to be pasteurized and bottled. It saved on work for all of them.

Looking across the river to Canada, Marie said, "Just think, Nellie, that's a foreign country over there."

"Do they talk English?" Nellie asked.

"Yes. They sound just like us. Except they say, 'Eh?' a lot."

Watching a fishing boat bobbing close to the Canadian side, Marie continued with her younger sister's education. "Isn't it strange that Canada is a foreign country and we can see it from here? But Ireland is far, far away, across the Atlantic Ocean. It took ten days for Ma and Pa to sail from Ireland to New York."

Both girls loved to hear the story about how their parents met when Pa was on his way from Ireland to Scotland to get a visa for America. He'd say, "I saw oranges in the window and they were a pretty sight, but when I walked into the store, the prettiest girl I'd ever seen was sitting there. She dropped a spool of thread on the floor and we bumped heads when we both bent down to pick it up"

Ma believed the Irish superstition that people who bumped heads would get married. "Faith, and didn't Pa and I prove 'tis true?" Ma had lots of superstitions. The Irish were known for their good luck, too, but it seemed to Marie that superstitions and leprechauns caused more bad luck.

Nellie sighed, "Isn't it romantic, Marie? How Pa traveled all the way back to Ireland to ask Ma to marry him?"

"But she didn't even know him. She only saw him once and then wrote to him for twenty-two years. Why did she write so long before hinting that 'he'd have company going back if he came for a visit?' I can't believe she waited that long."

"Pa was busy! He had to work and save money and find his land and then build his farm. She got engaged to somebody else, remember? What was his name?"

"Daniel. She didn't marry him because he liked to bet on the horses."

Nellie said, "She sure hates gambling. She has that tea set one of her brothers won. I like that tea set but Ma hates it."

She always says, "My brothers couldn't buy food with the tea sets they won at the races so they stole food from my store." Nellie giggled at Marie's imitation of Ma's voice.

"She gave her engagement ring from Daniel to her friend, Maggie."

Marie said, "Why does Ma give things away? She gave that pretty red butter dish with the silver frame and lid to Mrs. Withrow the other day. I liked that butter dish. Marie thought a moment. "She carried the dishes she brought from Ireland up the riverbank herself so they wouldn't get broken. Now she gives them away."

Nellie asked, "Do you think Ma was scared when she saw the Indian when they finally got to Pa's cabin? She climbed up the riverbank and there he was, that Indian named King, looking down at her."

"No, Pa told her about King, that he was living at the place and taking care of the livestock."

"Ma complains that the table was piled high with layers of newspapers sticky from syrup. The wood floors were a mess. King, his wife and three little papooses, and a couple dogs were enjoying a nice cozy cabin instead of a teepee."

"King's wife disappeared out the door before Ma could even talk to her. It's probably a good thing. I bet Ma lost her wicked Irish temper when she saw the mess that day!" The sisters giggled.

Marie said, "Ma scoured and cleaned. I wonder if she was disappointed when she saw such a little log cabin. When Pa told her that he'd built a new house, I think she expected something nicer."

"Ma doesn't get scared easily, does she Marie. What's that story about the prisoners coming here to help harvest the hay on the farm?"

"When I was a baby, Pa hurt his back when he was cutting down trees and he couldn't do much. Ma had to do all the milking. She left me in the house with Pa while she was outside doing all the chores herself. The sheriff was a friend of Pa's and he brought out the prisoners to help Ma with haying. She cooked for them and I guess they gave her lots of compliments. She said she told the Sheriff, 'I just don't know why you have these nice gentlemen in jail.'"

The girls flopped on their backs laughing.

When she could talk again, Marie said, "And she says, 'I left the two of them together in the house, but neither one could walk, so how could one help the other?'"

Wiping tears of laughter from her eyes, Nellie said, "What did Pa do if you cried?"

"I don't know. Probably told me that my mother was gone milking." And they roared again. She wrinkled her brow in thought. "Maybe we both crawled around on the floor and I thought we were playing."

A gust of wind suddenly whipped over the water and blew up dead leaves and twigs on the ground beside them. A memory popped into Marie's head. "Did you hear Ma crying last night?"

"No. Was she crying about Uncle Jim leaving?"

"Yes. I wish he'd stayed longer. He's really nice. He told Ma she should have let us play with those dolls he sent us instead of leaving them on top of the piano."

Nellie asked, "Didn't Ma write him a letter asking him to come?"

"Yes. She wrote that she had an abscess in her finger that could lead to blood poisoning. Know what she told him? 'I hope I don't die before I ever get to see you again.'"

"What's an abscess?"

"A bad infection. Remember when her finger was kind of red and full of pus and she put on Lysol poultices?"

Wrinkling her brow, Nellie thought a moment, then cried, "Oh, I remember now. She complained about it when she put her hands in water."

"I think Ma was a little nervous when she found out Uncle Jim was making the long train ride here to see her. By the time he got here, the abscess was healed. She was in perfect health."

"He wasn't mad, though. Uncle Jim hugged her when he got off the train, then he laughed and gave her another hug after she admitted she wasn't sick."

"Do you remember what she said, Nellie?" Marie imitated her mother's voice, "I may have exaggerated just a wee bit, but I was so lonesome I knew God would forgive a bit of a white lie."

Nellie giggled. "Uncle Jim teased her, said he was getting right back on the train."

Marie said, "If I lied like that I'd be sent down to the root cellar for punishment."

The sky was getting black. Marie looked down below where the wind was swirling across the river. A strong current normally rushing to the west was now reversing direction with waves skittering eastward, tossing white caps into the air. "The weather sure changed fast! Look how the river changed direction when the wind kicked up." Staring down at the river, she reflected a moment. "Our lives change too. Look at all the changes Ma's had in her life. Coming here and never seeing Ireland or her family again."

Tears gathered in Nellie's eyes. Her tender heart broke for her mother. Struck by another thought, she grabbed Marie's arm. "Promise you'll never leave me, Marie. Promise!"

"Life changes, Nellie. Just like the river. It depends on what happens when we grow up."

"No! You can't ever leave me. I don't want to ever be separated from you. Promise."

"All right, I promise! But we'd better run, it's going to rain."

Chapter 27

THE DORAN FAMILY
December 1924

"Christmas is going to be special this year!" Waving a letter, Ma was practically dancing. Marie had never seen her so happy. "Frank Doran is bringing his whole family to America. They'll be here for Christmas."

Before leaving Ireland, Annie had made Matt promise to allow her nephew Frank to live with them in America. Annie sent for him shortly after arriving in Goldville and Frank stayed with them until he went into the army. After injuring his knee, he was discharged with some compensation and he'd returned to Ireland.

Ever since the letter, Annie had a smile on her face as she bustled around making preparations for her sister and her family. The house had to be thoroughly cleaned. When they weren't cleaning, they were baking fruitcakes and cookies.

"Tell us their names again, Ma." Marie and Nellie couldn't believe they would have so many new cousins living by them.

"Well, Frank's mother is my sister Minnie. When Minnie moved to Scotland, my mother—my mother is your Grandma Susan Rice—wouldn't let Frank go. She didn't want her first grandson to go so far away. He lived with my mother and me for so long, he seemed like my own son. Faith, I missed him so bad your Pa let him come live with us in America."

"Who else is coming?" Marie asked.

"Minnie's husband, Uncle Tom. He'll be looking for work. He worked in a bathtub factory ever since they moved to Scotland, but now he lost his job because they closed down the factory. Millions of starving Irish have already crossed the Atlantic to find work in America. I was lucky. My mother owned Rice Produce store so we always had food. Your Pa's family was really poor and he was hungry most of the time.

"That's why he left Ireland, wasn't it, Ma?" Marie said.

"Yes. You girls don't have to worry about never having food. That's why Pa works so hard on this farm, to make sure you have enough to eat."

"Who are their kids?" Nellie asked, getting her mother back to the question.

"Minnie's oldest daughter, Annie—she's named after me—and her husband, John Casserty. Peggy and Kathleen are just a bit older than you are. And my godson Teddy. When Pa and I got married, I wouldn't leave for America without going to see Minnie. She had the baby baptized when we were there so we could be his godparents."

"Tell us about the fortune teller," Marie pleaded. She knew the story, but loved hearing it from Ma.

"My friend Maggie told me my fortune before your Pa came back to Ireland. Maggie was fey—she had the power to see into the future. Lots of Irish are fey. Maggie predicted, 'A short, dark-haired male is going to take a fair-haired lady out of this house and across water. They are going up the aisle of a church carrying something. Then they are going across a large body of water, and it will be a turbulent journey.'"

"And didn't it all come true?" Annie found it hard to believe herself. "We went across the Irish Sea to Scotland. There I was, carrying Teddy down the aisle to be baptized. We sailed to America across the Atlantic Ocean. 'Twas an awful journey with me sick the whole time. Ten days I was sick in bed and it didn't let up until we docked in New York." Ma stopped, lost in thought. Then she snapped, "Enough talking. Get those dishes done."

That night in bed, Marie whispered, "'Tis strange, Nellie. Frank's own mother left him behind in Ireland when she went to Scotland."

Nellie, who loved babies even more than Marie, found it hard to believe. "How could a mother leave her baby?"

"She did. Ma said so. Frank came from Ireland in March and I was born in July. He always bossed me around and was mean to me. I think he was jealous because I was born to Ma. I didn't cry when he went into the Army. Ma cried. She cried for days. I thought she'd never stop."

A letter arrived from Aunt Minnie giving the date they would be arriving on the train. Marie and Nellie looked at each other. "That's the night of the St Thomas Christmas party!"

After thinking a moment, Annie said, "'Twill work out perfectly. We'll meet them at the train depot at 6:00 o'clock and they can come to the party."

"Oh, I'm so glad we don't have to miss the party!" Nellie said.

Marie and Nellie were anxious to see their relatives, but not as anxious as Ma.

Marie had never seen her mother so excited. Singing Irish songs lustily, Annie had been busy baking batches of bread, fruitcakes, and cookies. Matt had butchered a pig and killed a dozen chickens. Annie had plucked the chickens, cleaned them, and fried them in bacon fat ready for tomorrow's dinner. The house was spotless.

It was time to go to the train depot. Marie and Nellie had been running in circles all day as Ma barked orders. Now, dressed in their best dresses for the Christmas party, they sat in the back seat trying to calm down from the excitement of the preparations. Ma fussed all the way to town. "Do you think Minnie will like it here? Will Tom be able to find a job? What if they missed the train? I hope they can find a house to live in. 'Twill be a crowd for our house."

"Do you think our cousins will like us?" Nellie asked her sister.

"Nellie, how many times have you asked me that?" Marie answered impatiently. "Why wouldn't they like us?"

At the train depot, Annie paced the length of the station.

Matt said, "Calm down, Annie. They'll soon be here."

Annie said, "I can't calm down. My sister is coming after all these years." She grabbed Matt's arm. "Maybe they can't get through because of the snowstorm last night. What if the train had a wreck?"

Luckily, the mournful Whooo-whoo of the train whistle could be heard in the distance and Annie became quiet as the tracks began to vibrate. Marie felt a strange melancholy from the sound and a sudden strange longing swept over her. She yearned to get on the train and ride to the reverberating rumble of the tracks.

The train stopped with a whoosh. The conductor hopped out and put down a small stool for the passengers to step on. Annie peered at each passenger stepping out of the train. Anxiously grabbing Matt's arm, she said, "I don't see her! What if they aren't on the train?"

Pa said, "Look! There she is!"

Minnie was barely off the train when Annie flung herself at her. The two sisters cried and hugged each other.

The rest of Minnie's family crowded around, and Annie hugged each of her sister's family while Aunt Minnie hugged the Donahues. Marie and Nellie had difficulty understanding their Scottish brogue, but Ma didn't have a problem.

Pa finally got everybody piled into his 1920 Chevrolet. It was a tight squeeze, with each lap occupied by another person, but Annie and Aunt Minnie talked nonstop all the way to the church.

Nellie giggled. "Can you understand them?"

"Not a single word," Marie whispered back.

The St. Thomas League hostesses for the event—Mrs. Withrow, Mrs. Kane, Mrs. Fogarty, and Mrs. McPartlin—fluttered around, excited at meeting Annie's relatives straight off the train from the old country.

Everybody coming in had to be introduced to the Scottish guests. Mrs. Withrow could barely be heard above the chattering as she tried to get people to sit down for the Christmas play. The third grade Mary casually held baby Jesus by an arm and Joseph fidgeted. Little fistfights were breaking out between angels and shepherds.

Mrs. Fogarty finally yelled above the buzzing, "The Christmas pageant is starting! Everybody sit down!"

Mrs. Kane and Mrs. McPartlin managed to get the small cast lined up again and the timeless Nativity story began with the Holy Family seated at the manger.

A cheerful but fearful-looking Santa handed out bags of candy after the play, although the angels had not been too angelic and Mary seemed rather a bored mother. Aunt Minnie asked Annie, "Do you think they would like to see Peggy and Kathleen dance the Highland Fling?"

Annie asked her friends sitting nearby and they all chorused excitedly, "Yes!"

Minnie pushed her daughters to the front of the room. "'Tis a Scottish folk dance," she explained. "Sure, and it got started with the wars. The men danced it after they won their battles."

Marie couldn't take her eyes off the dancers. Their feet flashed. They hopped and turned gracefully on one foot, flinging the other foot in front of the calf, then in back of it with one arm up in the air.

"Never have I seen dancing like that!" Pa shouted. The people clapped rhythmically, urging them on.

Marie promised herself, "I will learn to do that dance."

While the hostesses served fruit bread and desserts, people came to meet Aunt Minnie, complimenting her on her daughters' dancing. Minnie said, "Sure, and they dance even faster when the bagpipes are playing. The bagpipers are men wearing kilts and that's a sight in itself."

"Kilts! What do they wear under the kilts?"

Aunt Minnie giggled. "Sure, and 'tis their big secret." There were a few restrained giggles following that remark.

Marie, sitting next to Kathleen, asked shyly, "Would you teach me to dance like that?"

"Sure, and I will," Kathleen promised. "I love to do the dance."

Kathleen kept her word and every day, until the Dorans found their own house and moved out of the Donahue farm, she taught Marie and Nellie the steps to the lively jig. Marie practiced every day, determined to dance with as much flair as her cousins did.

Chapter 28

FALL EVENTS

August 1925

Marie brushed her damp hair back from her forehead as she stopped for a break. Sweat poured down her back. Haying was hard work, but it was threatening rain and Pa needed their help. Sniffing the air, she thought it had that special hint of fall, her favorite time of year. Her stomach growled as she thought about fresh vegetables from the garden.

"Corn-on-the-cob for supper tonight, Pa. Mmmm, my favorite. Except for eating peas in the garden."

"Not if your mother catches you," Pa reminded her. "Seems to me you like eating berries right off the bushes, too." She and Nellie had picked gallons of blueberries and wild raspberries. They sold the berries for ten cents a quart and Ma let them keep the money. Watching the berries fill up the pail was fun, and so was watching the coins count up in her bank. It was a good thing they'd saved some money, now that they were going to the state fair.

"You and Nellie can help Orley and me today," Pa had announced at breakfast. "The haying has to be done before we go to the Minnesota State Fair."

Nellie had entered her black and white Holstein in the 4-H competition at the county fair. An open field a couple blocks west of the downtown district served as the county fairground. The whole family was thrilled for Nellie when her heifer, Tillie, won a blue ribbon. County Agent Mark Abbott told Matt that only two animals were chosen from Koochiching County to go to the state fair and he should be very proud that Nellie's heifer was one of them. Mr. Abbott encouraged Matt to send Nellie and her calf to Minneapolis. "It will be a great experience."

Marie had heard her parents discussing the trip at night, always agreeing they couldn't afford to go. But three days after the county fair was over, Pa came in at lunchtime grinning. He announced: "Sure, and we're all going to Minneapolis!"

Ma slammed a bowl of potatoes on the table. "Matt Donahue, don't be joking with us! We already decided it would cost too much money." Marie and Nellie stood staring, their mouths and eyes wide open.

Pa said, "I know we can't afford it, but Nellie and Tillie deserve to go. Sure, and it will be an education for us all. I talked to Mr. Olson at the bank. He said this is a once-in-a-lifetime opportunity. Told me my word was good if I wanted to take out a loan from the bank." Pa beamed, proud of his reputation as an honest man.

"Oh, Pa!" Nellie cried, throwing her arms around her dad's neck. "We're really going to the state fair?" Nellie's face shone with excitement.

"Well," Pa laughed while untangling himself from her stranglehold. "You worked hard for the blue ribbon. I guess if you're willing to work a bit more, you deserve to go show her at the state fair. Besides, I've heard that Minneapolis is quite a city. 'Tis a good time to go see it." Matt hadn't completely lost his thirst for adventure.

Ma said, "I think Pa and I better discuss this trip a bit more." None of them ate much lunch. Marie was afraid she'd choke on her food with the big lump in her throat and she could see Nellie fighting back tears after Ma's discouraging statement.

The next day at lunch, Ma said, "Well, Pa and I discussed it some more and we will be going to Minneapolis to the state fair. They whooped with delight.

Daydreaming about the trip, Marie drove the horses up to the next stack of hay to be racked. She stood in the wagon to scatter the hay that Pa and Orley pitched up to her. When the wagon was full, she drove the horses to the barn where the hayfork would take it off the wagon and up into the barn to be stored.

While waiting for the wagon to be emptied, Marie asked Nellie, "Which do you like better, Fourth of July or Christmas?"

"Fourth of July. I love the parade! I love hearing the drums when the band goes by; I feel them pounding right down in my tummy. Plus, we get to stay in town for the whole day. What's yours?"

"Christmas. I like the story about Baby Jesus."

"I love that too, but on the Fourth there are so many people to see and we get to eat downtown."

Marie sighed as she thought about how much they packed into one day a year. "Remember the first time we went to the moving picture show? I didn't understand what it was all about because I couldn't read the captions, but I was fascinated by the black and white pictures moving on the screen."

"I can't understand how the sound comes out of the radio either. Remember that day Pa brought the radio home? It was hard to hear it."

"Well, if you would have kept quiet long enough for us to listen we might have been able to hear better."

"It sounds garbled," Nellie protested.

"Just think, school will be starting in a few weeks. I can hardly wait to see Stella and Winnie." Marie seldom saw her friends in the summer. "But I'm worried that junior high will be hard."

"Oh, you always get good marks, especially arithmetic. That's the hardest of all."

Marie liked counting things. Looking around to make sure that Orley was out of earshot, she said, "Tonight I'll count how many cobs of corn Orley eats."

Nellie giggled. "He eats a lot."

While driving the horses to the next stack of hay, Marie thought about their shopping trip to Burton Department Store. She told Nellie, "We're lucky that Ma lets us shop in the nicest store in town."

It had been fun trying on dresses and laughing when the dresses hung like gunnysacks on their thin frames. Marie couldn't resist trying on a pale pink dress with a white lace collar. One side of the skirt was gathered up at the hip. She felt very grown-up as she looked at herself in the mirror. "Oh, Ma, I love this dress."

"Sure, and it's a pretty dress but it wouldn't last the week without washing, not at all."

Nellie came out of the dressing room wearing a blue plaid shirtwaist that fit perfectly. "How does this look, Ma?"

"Good. We'll take it."

Reluctantly, Marie took off the pink dress and slipped into a practical green plaid. Both dresses were shirtwaists—small collars, buttons down to the waist, and tied in back. Ma checked the length. "Just below the knee. They won't need hemming."

Marie looked at Nellie's dress. "Couldn't I get blue for a change? I like blue, too."

Nellie immediately began to cry. Annie said, "Stop crying or I'll give you something to cry about." Marie silently wished she had a dime for every time her mother said that to Nellie.

Annie said, "Marie, you're getting that green one. Now both of you get dressed and be quiet or you won't get anything at all, not at all."

While Ma paid for the two dresses, Marie took one last feel of the soft pink dress. But she could only get one new dress and practical clothing was the fashion. During World War I, women began working at jobs that men had done. They needed serviceable clothing, not the frivolous dresses that had been the style. When Marie saw old pictures of the long dresses cinched at the waists she was glad her clothes allowed her to move. Ma still wore such a tight corset Marie didn't know how she could breathe.

Getting new school clothes was usually the most exciting thing that happened each fall. But this year they were going to the state fair. She'd hardly dared believe they were really going until Pa came home with the train tickets. He'd walked into the kitchen with a big grin on his face. After table grace, Ma said, "What are you grinning about?"

"I have a surprise." Paddy guessed candy, but Pa said, "Guess again." He patted his shirt. "'Tis right here in my pocket."

Nellie jumped up from her chair. "What?"

"Matt, quit teasing."

He put his hand into his pocket. "Train tickets!"

Marie was hot and dirty from haying all day, but working so hard was gratifying when the reward was going to Minneapolis.

Chapter 29

MINNESOTA STATE FAIR

September 1925

Whooo-whoo. The plaintive whistle announced that the train was coming. They'd arrived at International Falls Depot early to make sure they wouldn't miss the train. Marie's anticipation increased with the vibrations on the tracks and choo-choo-chooing of the brakes as the train slowed down. Marie felt a drumbeat deep inside her whole body that matched the train vibrations, her stomach rumbled, her blood rushed in her veins. The shiny black engine pulled to a stop in a swirl of black smoke and smell of coal. At long last, a trip on the train! She felt like she'd burst from so much anticipation.

Pa had brought them to the train station but he wasn't coming along. He planned to join them in two days, in time for the animal judging. He stood waving as the train pulled away.

They waved back. A sad look on Ma's face made Marie suddenly wonder if Ma could be scared about going without Pa. When Pa hugged Ma good-bye, Marie had heard him say: "Sure, and Mr. Abbott said he would take good care of you. Don't worry, Annie, you'll be OK." Brushing the thought away, Marie squirmed in her seat with excitement as the train started.

The Donahue family sat in two seats facing one another. Marie's heart raced in rhythm with the clickety clack of the train speeding down the tracks. The train had gradually picked up speed since the conductor called, "All Abooaard!" promptly at 6:00 p.m. In twelve hours, they'd be in Minneapolis.

Tears were trickling down Nellie's cheeks. "What's wrong?"

"Poor Tillie looked so scared. Why can't I stay with her?"

It hadn't been easy getting the calf into the train car. With Pa pushing while Nellie pulled, Tillie was finally settled in with the other mooing cows. Leaning out of the car, Nellie said, "I'm not leaving Tillie in here all by herself. I'll stay with her."

Ma said, "Absolutely not! It's a long ride to Minneapolis. You're sitting with us."

Nellie had given Tillie one last pat before crawling down from the train car.

Paddy chanted, "Cry baby Nellie. Cry baby Nellie."

Nellie slapped him and Paddy punched her on the arm, but Ma grabbed each of them. "Stop right now or we'll get off at the next stop."

County Agent Abbott stopped at their seat. "Everything OK, Annie?"

"Trying to calm down these restless kids." She reached for the picnic basket she'd stowed under the seat. "I think I'll feed them now. Want to join us?"

Mr. Abbott looked at the dish of fried chicken she held out. "Well, I might gnaw at a chicken leg." He sat down in an empty seat across the aisle.

While munching at his chicken, Mr. Abbott said, "Matt was telling me about that cow that ran away with the moose."

"Sure, and he tracked the two together but couldn't find them. Just as he'd predicted, the lovesick cow came back pregnant. But the calf only lived a couple days."

Paddy piped up, "It couldn't poop!"

Annie blushed but Mr. Abbott said matter-of-factly, "Yes, Matt said it was born without a rectum. I've heard of cows running off with moose before, and there's always something wrong with the calf. Too bad." Brushing his hands on his pants, the agent said,

"Well, I promised your husband I'd look after you. Let me know if you need anything."

Marie and Nellie giggled at how he swayed down the aisle as the train lurched down the tracks.

When the conductor came through announcing, "Minneapolis next stop" at 5:30 in the morning, they were all bone weary. Marie was glad that the long night was over. She wondered why she'd looked forward to such a long, boring ride. She didn't know which was worse, Paddy's fidgeting or Nellie's whining about Tillie. It was impossible to get much sleep with the train stopping hundreds of times for passengers to get on or off. Sometimes they seemed to be in the middle of nowhere. The most fun had been going to the huge jug of water and drinking out of paper cups that were shaped like ice cream cones.

As the train pulled into Great Northern Depot, they scrambled to get their belongings together. Ma said, "Hurry up. Mr. Abbott said there's a bus picking us up to take us to the fairgrounds in St. Paul. We have to follow him." She grabbed Paddy by the hand and pulled him along.

Marie held Nellie's hand tightly as they walked through the huge depot. "Just think, Nellie," she said, feeling overwhelmed, "We're three hundred miles from home and this is the largest city in Minnesota." Ma shoved them along behind Mr. Abbott. Men were loading up the livestock. Nellie forgot to worry about Tillie, she was so busy looking around at all the activity. As the bus pulled onto busy Minneapolis streets, they craned their necks trying to look out the windows at the tall skyscrapers and buildings. The roaring traffic made them frightened.

As they climbed off the bus at the exhibit barns, they stared in wonder at the rides towering in the sky; the music barely could be heard above the plaintive mooing from the cattle.

It was a busy day at the barns for all the 4-H exhibitors. Nellie scrubbed Tillie, polished her tail, and put a big blue ribbon on her. Paddy persistently pleaded to go to the fairgrounds until Ma finally said, "All right! Anything to shut you up. Nellie, we'll not be gone long."

Marie looked back at Nellie standing with her arm around Tillie's neck. She looked so lonely, Marie felt sorry for her. "Do you want me to stay with you, Nellie?"

"No. I'll be OK." Nellie said bravely, but Marie saw her lips quiver.

Walking around the fairgrounds, Marie said, "I've never seen so many people in my life!"

"Look at all the rides! Can we go on some?" Paddy pulled at his mother's hand.

Ma gave them each ten cents for a ride on the Ferris wheel. When the big wheel stopped at the top, Paddy rocked the car, making his sister sit rigidly in fright. "Stop, Paddy, we'll fall out! My stomach is doing somersaults!"

Fearlessly, Paddy leaned out. "Look how small the people are!"

As they hovered up at the very top, Marie felt sick when she looked down. It was a nice panoramic view, but it would be a long drop if she fell out. Swallowing hard, she prayed that she'd get down safely. "I wish we'd ridden on the merry-go-round instead. Look at all the pretty horses."

"Scaredy cat!"

Paddy begged for another ride, but Marie was glad that Ma shook her head. "We've been gone long enough. I have to check on Nellie." It was a relief to get away from the jostling crowds. Her ears ached from the clamor of music from the twirling rides, the screams from scared riders, and shouts from the barkers competing for customers. Greasy cooking odors hovering in the hot August air from the food booths were nauseating. When they reached the barns again, Marie tried to hold her breath because the stench of manure was so strong.

In the evening, the 4-H bus took them to the hotel. Excited about staying in a hotel for the first time, they ran through the long halls looking for their room number. Paddy and Nellie jumped up and down while Ma fumbled to unlock the door.

"Oh, it's so beautiful!" Nellie's mouth hung open. They all dropped their suitcases to gawk. Two big beds were covered with white chenille bedspreads and there was a long dresser with a mirror.

"Look at that big mirror! I can see almost all of me!" In the mirror at home, they had to stand on tiptoe to see their faces.

"Hey! Look at that fancy bathroom!" Paddy shouted.

They all crowded into the bathroom to touch the fluffy towels and shining faucets. Paddy flushed the toilet, and then they each took turns using the bathroom and flushing. Later, they all took baths. As Marie stretched out in the tub, she couldn't decide which was nicer—being able to spread out instead of being scrunched into a round tub or the luxury of hot water pouring out of faucets. When she got out she told Nellie, "That was the best bath I've ever had."

Saturday night baths at home were a lot of work. Marie and Nellie carried in pails of water and Ma heated the water on the wood stove. When the water was hot, she poured it into a round galvanized tub. They always fought about taking the first bath until Ma got mad and picked the lucky person. Pa was always last.

In the morning Nellie sighed, "Isn't it nice not have to go outside to use the outhouse, Ma?"

"Nellie, I have used an indoor bathroom before. Sure, 'tis nice. But ours is as clean as can be and plenty good." Ma sounded cross, but she surprised them when she added with a smile, "'Twill be the first thing on my list when your Pa finds that gold on our land!"

The next day, they ate lunch at a Catholic Church food booth. A friendly woman working there told Ma how to find the streetcar line outside the fairgrounds and where to get off downtown. "Go to Dayton's Department Store. You won't believe the merchandise in that store."

It was an exciting ride downtown. Even Paddy was too busy looking to bother his sisters. Their noses were pressed to the window as the streetcar followed the rails through the street, sparks sputtering from the electric lines overhead. "Look at how huge the buildings are. And they're right on top of each other."

"I didn't know there were so many people or so many motor cars in the whole world."

"How will we know when to get off?" Marie had been worrying about that too and was relieved when Paddy asked.

"The lady said Dayton's is on Nicollet and Eighth. Listen to the driver when he calls out the street names." Annie had taken the first seats behind the driver in case she needed help and was straining to listen each time the streetcar stopped. She couldn't understand what he said. Overhearing them, the driver turned around to say, "I'll let you know when to get off."

Each stop, when people crowded around waiting for the doors to open, they looked at the driver nervously. He'd shake his head no. Finally he yelled, "Niklet 'n' Eighth!"

When they didn't move, the driver looked at Ma. "Dayton's is right over there on that corner, Ma'am." They scrambled out quickly, worried they'd get squished in the whooshing doors that closed so quickly. Open-mouthed, they stood staring up at the tall buildings. Several years later, when she heard about the Foshay Tower built in 1929, Marie wondered why they wanted taller buildings than she had seen.

They stopped smack in the doorway of Dayton's Department Store, forcing people to walk around them as they stared in wide-eyed wonder. Marie said, "The store must be a hundred times bigger than Burton's at home."

Wandering past incredible displays of merchandise, Nellie said, "Look at all the pretty stuff!"

People were crowding into a small square-shaped room. A man in a uniform stood in front of a set of numbered buttons and asked, "What floor, please." Then he pushed a button, the door closed, and they heard a whirring noise.

"What's that?" Paddy asked.

"I know! It's an elevator! Our teacher told us about them," Marie said.

Paddy begged, "Can we ride in the elevator, Ma?"

"No. I don't trust it."

They watched it go up. When it came back down, people spilled out of it. "Please, Ma?" they begged. Paddy jumped up and down by her side. She frowned, but then shrugged her shoulders. "Sure, and I guess we can give it a try."

Marie's stomach did flip-flops. It wasn't as exciting as the Ferris wheel, but it still gave Marie a strange sensation to know that they were moving up in such a mysterious way. They rode to the top floor, and then walked around looking at the beautiful, expensive clothes. Back in the elevator, their stomachs did nose dives on the way down. Marie burst into giggles at the scared look on Nellie's face and Paddy's mouth opened wide. Ma's eyes looked ready to pop out of her head.

Ma herded them downstairs to the basement. "Things are supposed to be cheaper downstairs. I thought we'd look at winter coats." The two girls raced down the wide stairs excitedly with Paddy clumping hot on their heels.

Helplessly they walked through rows and rows of coats. When a clerk asked, "May I help you?" Ma turned to her thankfully. "Yes, please. I'm looking for winter coats for my daughters."

The saleslady helped them find the right sizes. After trying on a few coats, Nellie complained, "It's too hot! I don't want to try on any more."

"Well, 'tis your choice. If you don't want a new coat, we can leave."

Marie decided not to complain.

"Yeah, let's go!" Paddy pulled on his mother's hand, instantly ready to leave that hot forest of coats.

The saleslady pulled a blue coat out of the rack and held it up. Marie noticed that Nellie quickly forgot how hot she was as she slipped it on. "I love it!"

Frantically looking for a coat while Nellie pranced in front of the mirror and Paddy coaxed to go, Marie's heart beat fast as the clerk handed her a brown coat with a fake fur collar. Hoping it would fit, Marie held her breath as she slipped it on. It fit. Annie checked the price tag, and then asked if she liked it. Marie nodded her head, afraid to speak.

"I'll take them both," Annie said to the clerk. Marie and Nellie silently grinned at each other as they skipped along behind their mother to go back to the fairgrounds.

"Pa!" They jumped at Pa when they saw him waiting with Tillie the next morning. He'd gone directly to the livestock barn after getting off the train. Marie felt oddly relieved to have Pa here and Ma looked really happy. They helped Nellie get the Holstein ready for showing. Smoothing the blue ribbon that had gotten a little soiled, Nellie tied it around her heifer. Giving the calf a hug she said, "You're the prettiest one here, Tillie. C'mon now, we have to show you off to the judges."

Marie patted Tillie and said, "Good luck, Tillie."

The 4-H judges looked very serious. Nellie led her Holstein around the ring with the other junior livestock owners. Now and then a judge stopped an exhibitor so they could inspect an animal thoroughly. The judges huddled together discussing the livestock and then walked around posting the ribbons. A judge slapped a red ribbon on Tillie's stall. When Nellie realized that Tillie had received a prize ribbon, she jumped up and down blubbering, "Tillie won! Tillie won!" Tears running down her cheeks, Nellie gave Tillie a big hug.

"Tillie's a winner!" Marie shouted, blinking back her own tears. Paddy furtively gave the calf a proud pat. When Tillie had been complimented enough, Pa took them all for a ride on the Ferris wheel to celebrate. This time, Ma made sure Paddy didn't wiggle the car.

Taking the streetcar back to their hotel, they babbled to Pa about the fancy bathroom and begged to take baths for the banquet. Paddy said, "You can be first for a change, Pa! We can run more hot water each time!"

"No, I'm going to take a nap. Wake me up when all of you are done and I'll take mine."

"Only ten minutes each!" Ma ordered. "And I'll be first before you mess up the bathroom. But be quiet so Pa can get some sleep. Remember, he rode the train all night."

Marie and Nellie put on their new plaid school dresses and Paddy his new suit. Marie thought Ma looked pretty in her crisp white blouse and black skirt and Pa was handsome in his New York suit.

Mr. Abbott joined them in the lobby for the bus ride to the banquet at Nicollet Hotel. He told them that the Minneapolis Chamber of Commerce honored all the 4-H leaders and the exhibitors who had been awarded ribbons each year. He said proudly, "The 4-H is the only group that the Chamber of Commerce gives a banquet for."

"This room looks like something out of a fairy tale," Marie gasped as they entered the banquet room. Under glittering crystal chandeliers, silverware and china sparkled on tables draped in crisp white tablecloths. Napkins folded into triangles were tucked into glasses.

"Look at all those electric lights!" Nellie said. At home, they still had kerosene lanterns. Marie could tell from their expressions that her parents were as impressed with the luxurious surroundings as she was.

Pinching her arms as she held them crossed in front of her chest, Marie wondered how she could be so lucky. "This meal must be costing hundreds of dollars!" she whispered to Nellie.

A male waiter seated them at a table with another family. Waitresses poured water into crystal goblets, and then served salads in small bowls. Paddy said, "I hope this isn't all we're going to get. I'll be starvin' when I leave the table."

Waitresses brought plates piled high with pork and creamy mashed potatoes covered with brown gravy; Pa winked and said, "This is our kind of food, right Paddy?" A delicious chocolate ice cream sundae ended the meal. Although Marie felt a little nervous, it was exciting to be served in such elegance. She wanted to remember everything to tell her friends.

Nellie whispered, "What it would be like to be rich and live like this all the time?"

"I don't know, but this is the highlight of the trip," Marie whispered back.

Nellie disagreed vehemently. "No! Tillie's ribbon was the very best thing that happened!"

Still reeling from their unforgettable experiences, the next afternoon they boarded the train to go back home to reality. This time, nobody had to be coaxed to go to sleep.

During the half-hour stop at the Brainerd station, Marie drowsily thought about all she had seen and done. Already it seemed like a dream. Yet, she felt changed somehow—older and more mature. I'll bet there aren't many town kids who've been to Minneapolis and had such a grand banquet like we did at the Nicollet Hotel. Even if I do live in the country, I'm just as good as anybody else. I'm not going to be so shy and timid anymore, she resolved.

Chapter 30

MR. REGAN'S HOSPITALIZATION
March 1926

Two weeks after school started Pa announced at the supper table, "They took old man Regan to the hospital today."

Ma stopped pouring milk in Paddy's glass. "Poor man! What's wrong?"

"Not sure. Maybe his heart."

Marie thought Nellie looked as guilty as she felt. Nellie mouthed, "I'm glad we didn't eat Mr. Regan's pie."

Last summer, she and Nellie had eaten some of the pie that Ma was sending to their two bachelor neighbors, Mr. Regan and Mr. McGowan. Ma had put two pieces of pie on each plate and told them to walk carefully so they wouldn't drop the pie. They were barely out of the driveway when Nellie had asked Marie, "Can't we eat one piece of pie?"

The warm raspberry pie smelled so good. Marie said, "Let's take one little bite out of Mr. McGowan's pie." But they couldn't stop eating and ate one whole slice. Sitting on a rock beside the road, they looked guiltily at the messy plate showing evidence of another slice of pie.

"Let's take pie to Mr. Regan, but not to Mr. McGowan. We don't like Mr. McGowan anyway." They gobbled up Mr. McGowan's second piece of pie.

Just as they were wiping off their faces, Paddy had jumped out at them. Seeing the empty plate and the pie on their faces he'd yelled, "You ate that pie. I'm going to tell Ma!" Paddy raced away.

The sisters knew they were in trouble and stayed a while visiting with Mr. Regan. When he offered them some pie, they refused. When they got home, Ma was waiting for them with a switch. After using the switch on them, she warned: "You two won't get any money for Fourth of July. I can't believe you ate that pie."

Every day they worried. What fun would it be on the Fourth without any money? It was such a treat to actually be able to look at everything and pick out something to buy. Apparently their mother had forgotten the incident because she didn't mention her threat when Pa gave them a penny for each potato bug they'd picked. They couldn't believe it when Ma didn't say anything, especially when Pa gave them another fifty cents for picking mustard; they felt rich.

Concerned now about Mr. Regan, Marie asked, "Did it happen while he was chopping wood?" Marie asked.

Pa gave her a puzzled look. "Why do you ask that?"

"He works hard at chopping wood and has the neatest woodpile. His kindling is always perfect."

"Sure, and do I have time to inspect my neighbor's kindling wood?"

"I must go visit him. I heard one of the nuns from the school, Sister Mary, is in the hospital too. I can visit her too. Tomorrow's Saturday. You girls get your cleaning done quickly tomorrow. Marie can go with me to the hospital. Nellie can stay with Paddy."

"Can't I go too?" Nellie asked.

"No. You stay with Paddy."

When Pa left on his afternoon delivery trip to town, Ma and Marie rode in with him. It was a warm day and it felt good to relax after working hard all morning.

"Be back to pick you up in about an hour," he said to Annie as she and Marie climbed out of the car.

Marie sniffed the clean antiseptic smell as they walked into the hospital. Nurses wore white starched uniforms that rustled as they hurried through the halls and when Ma stopped a nurse to ask directions to Mr. Regan's room, Marie stared in fascination at the quaint-looking cap perched on her head. She wondered how it stayed on her head.

Looking pale and small in the bed, Mr. Regan acted embarrassed and didn't seem to know what to say, but after Ma chatted for a while he seemed to relax.

Marie told him, "Paddy went to the State Fair with his prize Guernsey this year. Remember, last year Nellie was awarded a trip for her calf, Tillie, and we all went? But Paddy got to go all alone."

Annie said, "County Agent Abbott went, and a couple 4-H leaders. Margaret Earley had a prize-winning calf too, so we asked her to watch out for Paddy. I told her to make sure he took a bath and changed his shirt. But when they came back Margaret told me she didn't see Paddy at all the whole time they were there! I think he stayed out of her way on purpose because he knew I'd asked her to watch out for him. Who knows what kind of mischief he got into!" Mr. Regan smiled.

Father Labonte came in. Ma introduced the Catholic priest to Mr. Regan and they all said a prayer for Mr. Regan with the priest. "Father, is Sister Mary still here?"

"That she is. I'm on my way to see her."

"I'll go along with you. Marie, you stay and visit with Mr. Regan. Help him with that ice cream." Mr. Regan was ignoring the dish of melting ice cream the nurse had left for his afternoon snack.

Marie sat down in the chair beside the bed that her mother vacated. Picking up the ice cream dish and spoon, she said, "Mr. Regan, it looks like good strawberry ice cream. Here, taste it."

"Don't want any."

"Sure you do. It's good for you. Open your mouth—here it comes."

Mr. Regan opened his mouth and Marie nervously put in a small spoonful of the ice cream. She talked about school while she spooned in the ice cream. "I'm writing a report on Rainy Lake City. Pa worked there, did you know that?"

"He told me."

"That's why he named his land Goldville. After the gold."

"Yup." She had the spoon waiting at his lips and as soon as he finished speaking, she slipped it into his mouth.

"Pa has a chunk of fool's gold. I've been reading all about gold for my report and the real name for fool's gold is Iron Pyrite. Pyrite is more yellow than real gold and shinier, like the nugget that Pa has. Did you ever work in the gold mines?"

"Nope. They were closed before I came."

A nurse came in shaking a thermometer. "I see you have a special nurse here." Noticing the ice cream was all gone, she said, "Thank you for helping him eat his ice cream. He hasn't been eating much. He wants to go home, but without a wife to take care of him, we think he should stay here a few more days."

Ma came bustling back in just then. "Sure and I'll send food over, but maybe a few days more won't hurt him. Well, Pa must be here by now. 'Tis time to get home and get supper ready. You get well, now, Mr. Regan."

Marie felt sorry for Mr. Regan lying in bed so listlessly as she waved good-bye.

Sunday night the phone rang. Ma answered and exclaimed, "The poor man. I wonder if he has any next of kin?"

"Poor old Mr. Regan died today," she said after hanging up.

Marie felt as though Paddy had punched her in the stomach. *Is it my fault he died? Did he die because I fed him ice cream? Maybe he shouldn't have eaten it. He didn't really want it, but I insisted and shoved it in. Maybe I fed him too fast.* When they went to bed, Marie and Nellie said a prayer for Mr. Regan and cried.

Marie could not blot out the picture of herself at Mr. Regan's bedside. As she tossed and turned, she heard herself repeating over and over, "Open your mouth, Mr. Regan." Anguish and guilt pounded at her head. Killing was a mortal sin! How could she confess such a monumental sin to the priest on Saturday? She tossed and turned until she finally fell into a fitful sleep. Whenever she awoke, she felt hot and sweaty at the same time.

Chapter 31

APPENDICITIS ATTACK
March 1926

Pain in her side distracted Marie from worrying about Mr. Regan the next morning. But she forced herself to get dressed and start breakfast. After school, she limped into the kitchen holding her side. "Ma, I've had a backache all day. I don't feel good."

Looking distracted, Ma ignored her. "Did you drink milk from down in the well?"

"No."

"Nellie, did you?"

"No, I never get milk out of the well."

"Paddy?"

"Nope, not me. Maybe Indians are lurking about. You said you saw Indians by the well once."

"That was a long time ago when King stopped by to see Pa with a couple of his friends. Sure, and didn't it give me a start, not recognizing him. I'd not seen him since the first day I got here. But King disappeared a few years ago. Pa thinks he moved back with his tribe after everybody deserted Rainy Lake City."

Nellie said, "Maybe our leprechauns drank the milk?"

"Forget leprechauns, somebody has been around here. The pail was full yesterday. Now it's nearly gone. I don't think Pa drank it, but remind me to ask him tonight. There's just enough for the chocolate cake I started." Annie went back to stirring her batter. She muttered, "I planned to make a cream sauce for the vegetables, but I'll just put butter on them."

Paddy said, "Hey, I just remembered. I saw Orley by the well this morning when we left for school. He probably drank the milk."

"Well, go ask him, Paddy. I want to know. Marie, go down to the cellar and get some potatoes and carrots. Nellie, go pick beans. Don't forget to change your clothes first."

The girls didn't need reminding to change to their every-day work dresses and aprons. Their serge school clothes needed special care because they were washed only once or twice a year and they wanted them to stay nice.

Down in the dark and dirty root cellar, Marie bent over to pick potatoes out of the bin. The scene of herself feeding Mr. Regan ice cream as he lay in his hospital bed flashed through her mind. Although she'd managed to close her mind to the heavy burden of guilt while busy at school, every now and then her conscience blasted at her.

With her pan of potatoes in her hands, she looked around for the carrots. Suddenly she doubled over with pain in her side. The pan of potatoes fell to the floor as she grabbed her side. The pain circled to her back. Was God punishing her for Mr. Regan's death? She crawled up the stairs and gasped weakly, "Ma."

Annie came running to help her daughter, who had broken out in a cold sweat. She tucked her into bed and bathed her face with a cool cloth.

Annie forgot to mention the missing milk to Matt that night. She was concerned about Marie as she became sicker and her fever rose higher.

"Ma, my side hurts but 'tis worse in my back. I'm so hot." Afraid that Marie would keep Nellie awake, she made a bed for her on the davenport. Annie was up and down all night soothing Marie as she tossed back and forth on the bed. In the morning Annie said, "Matt, we have to take Marie to the doctor. Let's take her to that new woman doctor." Dr. Mary Ghostley, in spite of the community's shock at a female doctor, was highly respected for her skill, especially by the women.

Dr. Mary examined Marie, who flinched whenever she touched her abdomen and back. Dr. Mary said, "I'm really puzzled. It acts like appendix, but I don't know why her back is hurting. I'm worried about her. Take her home and keep her quiet while I think about this."

The phone was ringing when they walked into the house. It was Dr. Mary. "Bring Marie to the hospital right away. I'm sure it must be appendicitis and I'm anxious to do surgery before the appendix bursts."

Pa drove carefully to avoid the bumps and then carried her into Northern Minnesota Hospital. A nurse rushed ahead to pull back the covers on a bed and Pa gently lowered her down.

Marie hated saying good-bye to Ma and Pa but she knew her parents had chores waiting at home. "I'll be back first thing in the morning, Marie, and I'll pray the rosary for you tonight," Ma said, patting her head.

As she drifted off to sleep, Marie prayed that she wouldn't die in the hospital like Mr. Regan. Groggy as she was from medication in the morning, Marie was relieved to see Ma's face bending down to give her a kiss before she was wheeled away to the operating room. "Sure, and I've got my beads and will be saying the Rosary again."

Annie paced the floor. What was taking so long? Dr. Mary said the operation would only take about an hour. When she finally came out of the operating room two hours and forty-five minutes later, the doctor looked as exhausted as Annie felt. "We're lucky that appendix didn't burst. I've never seen anything like it. The appendix somehow attached itself to her back. That's why the poor girl was having so much back pain."

"Sure, and now that I think of it, she has complained of her back now and then. But I thought it might be from working in the garden."

"It was a narrow escape. Not only was the appendix bad. I found cysts on both ovaries. I had to cut away a bit of each ovary. It must have been the luck of the Irish that pulled her through this one!"

"Her ovaries! Will she be able to have children?"

"Oh, yes. She could have a dozen." Annie did not think it would be possible. Many times through the years, she warned Marie, "You better not expect to have children."

Marie was still asleep when she was wheeled back to her room on the gurney. She gradually started waking up, moaning, and dropping back to sleep. The more she awakened, the sicker she became. Then she started retching. The nausea finally subsided and Annie tried to make her drink water but she turned her face away. Ma coaxed, "Just a little sip."

Giving in, Marie took a sip and threw up. A nurse came in to help, saying, "It's the ether—the anesthesia that put her to sleep for the operation. It makes some people more nauseated than others."

Looking concerned when she made hospital rounds the next morning, Dr. Mary said, "Marie, you have to drink more water."

Beckoning to Annie, Dr. Mary walked into the hallway. "Annie, we'll have to get liquids into her; otherwise, we'll need to insert a tube into her rectum and give her sugar water."

Annie spent several hours a day at the hospital caring for her daughter. Marie appreciated it most of the time. She just wished Ma would quit telling every nurse and every visitor that came into the room about how seasick she'd been on her honeymoon: "Sure, for ten days on that boat coming to America I laid in my bunk desperately sick. Not a bit of food could I eat. Not Matt. No, and wasn't he having a grand old time visiting with the captain of the ship."

When Dr. Mary gave her permission to eat, the thought of food made Marie's stomach churn, but the nurses praised her when she finally forced herself to eat a few crackers and spoonfuls of Jell-O.

Lying in bed watching the nurses rush up and down the hall to make patients comfortable, she daydreamed about becoming a nurse. Most of the nurses fussed over her and made her feel special, but her favorite was Miss Lindeman. She stopped often to check on her, plump her pillows, or bring her extra juice. She showed her how she clamped her cap down with hairpins. When Miss Lindeman was giving her a bed bath, Marie confided, "I'm going to be a dancer. My cousins from Scotland taught me the Highland Fling and the Irish dances. But maybe I should be a nurse instead."

Miss Lindeman said, "I do like helping people. But it's a hard job with lots of lifting and cleaning up messes. It isn't always pleasant."

Sniffing in the smell of disinfectants Marie said, "I even like the hospital smell. I think a hospital would be a good place to work. But I have lots of time to make up my mind."

"Yes, you certainly do. But you'd make a good nurse, I can tell."

It was an effort for Marie to walk from the bed to the chair while Miss Lindeman held onto her arm. "I'm so weak! I can't even stand up straight," she moaned.

"It takes time to recover, Marie. Don't worry, you'll heal. You'll be back at school like nothing happened."

While watching the nurse make neat hospital corners on her bed, Marie said, "Can ice cream make people die?"

"Not that I know of," Miss Lindeman said.

Taking a deep breath, Marie's words tumbled out on top of each before she could lose courage. "What if a man was in the hospital and somebody fed him ice cream when he didn't want it and then he died?"

"It wouldn't have been the ice cream. Whatever he was in the hospital for made him die. Patients often are very sick and die." The nurse studied her young patient, wondering why she'd asked such a strange question. She wanted to question her more, but Marie looked tired and she said, "Now, it's back into bed for you, young lady."

With Miss Lindeman helping her, Marie scooted back into her bed. Although exhausted, she felt like a ton of bricks had been removed from her shoulders. With a clear conscience she relaxed and soon dozed off. Her last thought was, "I won't have to confess to the priest after all."

Eleven days after surgery, Marie was overjoyed to leave the hospital. She was lonesome for Nellie; surprisingly, she even missed Paddy.

She took big gulps of fresh air. Although it still had a bite to it, there still was a promise of spring. She gazed hungrily out the car window on the ride home. One of March's surprise snowstorms last night had cloaked the trees with fresh white snow. She absorbed the magical scene of frosted flakes drifting lightly from trees. Pa was driving in two tracks through pristine snow.

Nellie and Paddy hung back wide-eyed as Pa helped her through the door. Nellie, of course, nearly smothered her with concern. The surprise was her brother. Paddy popped into her room often to check on her, asking if she needed something, running to get things for her. Marie couldn't believe her younger brother was being so attentive.

Chapter 32

MYSTERIOUS DISAPPEARANCE

1926

Her mother's screech woke her. Not fully recovered yet, Marie was napping in her room and when she opened her eyes, Ma stood over her looking ready to explode. "Pa's gold nugget is missing!"

"It is?"

"Help me look for it. I was dusting in the front room and it's gone from the table. Maybe it fell off and rolled under the furniture."

Crawling on her hands and knees, Marie looked under all the furniture. Her stomach felt like it had turned to stone and she didn't want her mother to see her face, afraid her mother would guess that she knew something. Marie ran around the house, busily poking into corners, behind furniture and under furniture. "Nothing, Ma."

The minute Ma went outside, Marie ran to her school bag. She'd forgotten that she'd brought the nugget to school. She hadn't asked permission, expecting to put it back before anybody noticed. It was the day she'd had her appendicitis attack.

She dumped everything out of the bag. Frantically feeling for something hard in the pile, she scattered books and paper. Punching the bag produced nothing. No gold nugget. Waves of fear clutching at her stomach were as nauseating as ether. The appendix should have killed me. Ma and Pa will kill me now, for sure.

Ma's rosary. Ma always gets out the beads when she needs to pray for something special. Marie darted into her parents' bedroom and plucked the rosary beads off the chest. Heart pounding, clenching the beads tightly in her sweaty fist, she scampered to her room. "Hail Mary, full of grace. Please help me find Pa's gold. Jesus, Mary, and Joseph, please help me find it before I get a whipping. I didn't mean to steal it, honest. I just borrowed it to show my teacher. I was going to put it back. Hail Mary . . ."

The door slammed. Ma was talking and then Pa shouted, "Where could it have gone, woman?"

Ma yelled back, "Don't you blame me, Matt Donahue. I found it missing; I didn't take it. Sure, and don't I have enough to do without checking your old rock every day?" Marie put the pillow over her head, praying harder.

Pa slammed out the door.

Marie felt paralyzed with fear. She debated whether she should confess. Ma banged around the kitchen all day, muttering to herself. She dropped a fork and said, "Who could be coming to visit today? A fork means it will be a lady visitor." But the superstition was wrong—nobody came to visit.

Supper was a silent meal. Ma wasn't talking to Pa. Marie knew the silence might last a few days. What was she going to do? Where had she lost Pa's nugget? The kids at school had been really impressed with it. Had one of them stolen it? Who had admired it the most? She ran a few suspects through her mind, but dismissed them all.

Chapter 33

A Bad Haircut

Spring 1927

Easter Saturday after the chores were done, Ma put a chair in the yard for Paddy to sit in while Orley cut his hair. Marie anxiously waited for her turn. She'd tried arguing with Ma that she didn't want the hired hand to cut her hair. Orley gave her the creeps and she avoided him as much as possible. He was always sneaking up on her and Nellie and she hated the way he looked at her with his beady eyes. Neither of the girls liked him, but Paddy thought he was great because he let him sit on his lap and drive the tractor. When she mentioned that she didn't like Orley, Ma said, "He's big and strong and a good hired hand. Pa needs him."

Last week Paddy was teasing her, calling her a sack of deer horns because she was skinny. Orley heard him and said, "Leave your sister alone. She looks good." Now, whenever she was near him, she felt queasy.

"Both of you shut up!" she yelled before running to the house. She looked at him closely now as he cut Paddy's hair, but Orley didn't show signs of being mad at her for yelling. Still, she felt uneasy.

When Paddy's haircut was done, Ma shook out the towel and motioned Marie to sit in the chair.

Thumping down heavily, as though she weighed a ton, she gave Ma a pleading look. Ma paid no attention. "Why do I have to get my hair cut? Nellie isn't getting hers cut."

"Nellie's hair curls nice when I put in rag curls. When your hair is too long, it just hangs."

Marie suddenly remembered something. "Orley, did Ma ask you about drinking milk from the well?"

"What are you talking about?"

"The day I got sick and went to the hospital Ma said that some milk was missing. Paddy saw you by the well. Did you drink it? Did you?"

"How can I remember back that far? Maybe I did, maybe I didn't."

"Well, Ma needed it for creamed vegetables. She was mad at us for drinking it." I'll give Orley something to worry about, she thought smugly.

Head down, watching her hair falling in black clumps to the ground, she began to fidget. "Aren't you done yet? How much are you cutting?"

Orley grunted, "Nearly done. I have to get it even."

Finally, Orley let her out of the chair. She felt in back of her head. Screaming she ran into the house and into her bedroom to look in the mirror. The sight in the mirror was even worse. "I look like a boy! It's shorter than Paddy's!" Hurling herself on the bed, she wailed, "I'm not going to school looking like this!"

She heard Ma scolding Orley, but that didn't lessen her anguish. Marie told Nellie, "I know he cut it like a boy's to embarrass me."

An hour later she crept from her damp pillow to dig into her closet. She found a brown cloche that covered her entire head. I'll be wearing that hat all day in school for sure!

When Nellie came to bed, Marie said, "I haven't felt this unhappy about going to school since the day the teacher caught me and Verona Dardis jumping over the desks during recess. After that, Verona and I had to stand in the front of the line whenever we lined up to go out for recess or to the bathroom. It was embarrassing."

Nellie said, "I remember how mad Ma got at you. How did she find out?"

"I don't know. I'd hoped she wouldn't hear about it. I knew what my punishment would be. The root cellar. I hate that place, so dirty and scary. You're always crying so hard, she doesn't make you go down there as often as me." Just thinking about the root cellar made Marie shiver and she cuddled up next to Nellie.

Marie woke with a start in the middle of the night. A memory pecked at her mind like a chicken pecking feed. With eyes tightly shut, she visualized back to the day she took the fool's gold to school for her report, retracing the entire day step-by-step. She vividly recalled returning to her desk and putting the nugget back into her school bag. When she got home she got so sick that Ma and Pa loaded her into the back of the car. Ma said, "Here, put this in the house." It was her school bag; she'd left it in the car. Who did Ma hand it to? Nellie? She was crying as usual. Paddy? No, he was standing on the opposite side of the car. Orley? Yes! Ma picked up the bag and said, "Put this in the house." Orley! Orley must have looked through her bag, found the nugget of fool's gold and thought it was real gold.

Marie fell asleep hatching a plan.

Chapter 34

EASTER SUNDAY
1926

The cloche covered her head. Standing on tiptoes to check herself in the mirror, Marie was relieved that it covered the bad haircut. As they left for early morning Easter Sunrise Mass, Nellie said, "That hat looks nice on you, Marie."

"Good thing it does. I'll be wearing it for a while."

"Well, it looks good with your new dress. Although I don't know how many people will see us in our new clothes at 6:00 in the morning," Nellie said.

Ma made Orley go to Mass with them, but he stayed in town to visit friends, planning to get a ride home later. Ma disappeared outside to hide Easter eggs while Marie and Nellie were doing breakfast dishes. As she thought about sneaking into Orley's room, Marie felt nauseous. His room was in the milk shed and Ma would wonder why she was going in there. What if Ma caught her in Orley's room? What if Orley came back while she was in there? She didn't know which would be worse.

Concentrating on her thoughts about searching Orley's room, she dropped a cup. Hands still in the sink, she began to cry. Surprised, Nellie bent down to pick up the cup. "Just the handle broke. Don't cry. Maybe Ma won't be too mad."

"Nellie, listen. I think Orley might have that gold nugget of Pa's. I thought about it last night and I have a plan. Keep Ma busy because I want to search his room."

Nellie's eyes got almost as big as the teacup. "Orley took it?"

"I think so. He acted strange when he cut my hair—like he was guilty of something. And look how he cut it. I think he did it deliberately."

"Come find the eggs!" Ma yelled. Paddy was already racing toward the barn. Walking nonchalantly toward the milk shed, Marie watched until her mother moved out of sight before slipping quickly into the shed and Orley's room.

Swallowing the fear in her throat, she closed the door quickly and scanned the room. The lone chair was strewn with clothes and a chest beside the unmade bed was also stacked with clothes. The chest had four drawers and she ran over to open them. She felt nothing hard as she groped through the tangle of clothes in the first two drawers.

Impatiently she yanked open the third drawer. Empty. Where did he put it? Was I wrong about Orley? She looked around in a panic, her heart pounding. There weren't any other cupboards or closets, just a few open shelves crammed haphazardly with Orley's meager possessions.

She heard Ma yelling. "Marie! Where are you!"

"Marie! I bet I found more eggs than you!" Paddy shouted.

With a feeling of despair, she jerked open the bottom drawer. The smell of dirty clothes gagged her. She wanted to slam the drawer shut, but instead plunged her hand around the sides. In the back corner of the drawer, she felt something that felt like a rock. Shoving the clothes aside, she snatched out the object.

Marie rushed outside clutching Pa's gold nugget in her fist. Nellie and Paddy were counting their eggs. Heart racing fast, she walked over to Ma, Marie held out her hand. Staring, Ma asked, "Where did you find it?"

"In Orley's room."

"Matt! Matt!" Pa came running out of the barn and Ma held up the chunk of fool's gold. "Marie found your gold rock in Orley's room!"

Pa took the nugget, turning it over before turning on Marie. "What were you doing in Orley's room?"

"I thought he might have it."

Pa said, "I can't believe Orley came in and stole it out of our front room"

"You're just trying to get back at him for cutting your hair so terrible," Paddy said with a big smirk on his face.

Marie took a deep breath for courage. "I'm not. I think Orley took it out of my school bag."

"What was it doing in your school bag?" Ma's glare made Marie want to run.

"I took it to school to show to the class when I gave my report on Rainy Lake City. Remember? I wrote about Pa . . ."

"You took Pa's nugget!"

"I didn't think about using it for my report until morning and grabbed it on the way to school. I showed them the gold when I gave my report. I would have put it back that night, but I got sick. That's when I had to have my appendix out. Remember how sick I got?" Looking at Ma's stormy face, Marie could see that Ma was not going to feel sorry for her. She knew she was in trouble. She felt a whack on her backside.

"You've been taught not to steal. That was stealing. Do you understand that? How could you do such a thing? I cannot believe my daughter would steal. My daughter, stealing."

"I wasn't stealing." Marie's bottom lip stuck out defensively.

At the next swat, a sob escaped. She was too old to get a spanking.

"Get to your room," Pa said,

Marie ran into the house. Flopping on her bed, she sobbed until she was exhausted. She knew she'd be punished. Her parents always talked about honesty. Pa never cheated any of his customers. Ma complained that he let his customers cheat him, but Pa always said, "If they could afford to pay, they would."

The door slammed as Pa went out. Marie pretended to be asleep but Ma wasn't fooled. "Sure, and you did it now, didn't you. It was you who took the gold nugget. And always pretending to look for it.

You lost it. I think Paddy's right—you're blaming Orley because he gave you that terrible haircut."

"No! I remember putting it in my school bag. Remember how you handed the bag to Orley when you were taking me to the hospital? Remember that?"

A strange expression crossed her mother's face; Marie was sure she'd remembered. Annie gave no hint on whether she did, saying, "You were stealing when you took something that belonged to Pa. And lying, too, when you didn't tell us you had taken it." Giving Marie a slap on her leg, Annie left the room.

Exhausted from crying, Marie dozed. She woke up to hear her parents discussing her punishment. "She'll have to go to reform school!" Ma said.

Pa said, "'Tisn't that a bit harsh? She meant to put it back."

"She has to be taught a lesson. She'll learn not to steal at reform school."

"Oh, no! Don't send her to reform school!" Nellie wailed.

Marie felt a surge of love for Nellie. In spite of her terror, she dashed out of the bedroom. "Please don't send me away. Please! I'll never take anything again! I was going to put it right back, honest. I wasn't stealing it! Orley stole it."

"Get back to your room."

"I'll think about what to do with her." Pa slammed the door. Burying her head in the pillow, she hoped her mother wouldn't come back into the bedroom.

Muttering as she prepared Easter dinner, Annie said loud enough for Marie to hear: "She didn't say a word when we were upset about that gold being gone. She even helped me look for it. That's how dishonest she was about the whole thing. Never said one word. Lying and stealing. 'Tis reform school for her."

Nellie quietly sneaked into the bedroom, patted Marie tenderly and quickly left. Gratitude for her sister choked her as tears slid silently down her chapped cheeks. Trembling, Marie prayed, "Please, God, don't let them send me to reform school. I'll never do anything bad again. Please, God."

"Marie, get out here and set the table! Company will be here soon."

Jumping off the bed, Marie ran out to the kitchen. After setting the table, Marie rinsed her flushed face in cold water wishing she could stay in bed. The entire meal Marie was stiff with fear, picking at her food. Waiting for somebody to bring up her misconduct, she felt like running from the table. But not even Paddy mentioned the missing gold nugget. She couldn't believe he didn't blurt it out.

After their company left, Marie and Nellie did dishes while Ma and Pa relaxed in the front room. Headlights came into the driveway. Ma looked out the window and said, "Must be Orley."

Marie felt glued to the floor, but Pa shot out the door. They heard the two men shouting in the driveway, and then a light went on in Orley's room. They sat quietly as mice, waiting. Marie wondered if Ma could hear her heart thumping. Pa didn't come in. Fifteen minutes later an engine started; lights went down the driveway.

Paddy sniffed, "I liked Orley. He let me drive the tractor with him."

Pa's face was red as a beet when he came back into the house. Ma said, "Now who will help you with the work around here?"

"I'll have to hire somebody else," Pa said curtly.

Everybody went to bed in silence. Marie did more praying than sleeping.

Chapter 35

A DARK EASTER MONDAY

1926

Marie, her face still swollen from crying, kneeled in front of her mother sitting at the breakfast table. "Please, Ma, don't send me to reform school," she begged.

Seated in their chairs, Nellie wailed and even Paddy begged not to send her away. Pa relented first. "We'll not be sending you away, Marie."

Ma didn't give in so easily. "You'll not be getting off free. Down in the root cellar with you."

Stooped as an old lady, Marie shuffled into the living room to the root cellar door, pulled it open, and groped her way down the two steps to the dirt floor. The dank cellar had been dug under the original one-room shack Pa first put up. Spiders and mice scurried around. Whenever Ma wanted her to go down to retrieve vegetables or fruit, she went down slowly, grabbed whatever she'd been told to get, and raced back up the stairs, her heart in her throat.

Marie huddled on the second step from the floor, thinking that spot was the safest place from the crawly creatures living in there. Her arms wound around her legs, holding them close to her body. *Easter's supposed to be joyful but this year it seems like Good Friday never ended.* Reflecting on the "Passion of our Lord Jesus Christ" presented at Good Friday's church service, she pictured Christ praying on his knees in the garden. Now she had a small glimmer of the agony He'd gone through. "When I get let out of this place, it will be like rising from the dead and the Resurrection. Ma is mean. She says her own mother was a lot stricter, but I don't know how Grandma Rice could have been worse than Ma. I know one thing. I'll never be as bad tempered with my kids."

It seemed like she was down there for hours before Ma finally opened the door to let her out. When she looked at the clock in the kitchen, it was only fifteen minutes.

Chapter 36

FOURTH OF JULY
1926

Marie and Nellie shot out of bed the minute they heard Ma and Pa in the kitchen. "Fourth of July is the best day in the whole year, isn't it Marie?"

Her disgrace was over. Marie was grateful to be enjoying the day with her family and not away at reform school. It seemed an act of forgiveness when Pa paid her for picking potato bugs—a penny a bug—and fifty cents for picking mustard.

Paddy came out of his bedroom rubbing his eyes while Marie was busy cooking breakfast. "Paddy, will you help out in the barn this morning?"

"That's Nellie's job."

"Nellie and I have to pick wild blue Iris for Mrs. Withrow. If she doesn't have to go out in the barn we can get started earlier so we're not late for the parade."

"You mean blue flags? Why does Mrs. Withrow want a bunch of blue flags?"

"She's decorating her car for the parade. Ma said we'd pick the blue flags for her. Remember last year? She was in the parade with her car all decorated with flowers?" Mrs. Withrow was active in community affairs and loved driving her car in the parade.

Paddy was not happy about going out to the barn. "Dr. Withrow will pay us for the flowers. We'll give you some of the money."

"How much?"

"Well, I don't know how much we're going to get! Go do the chores."

"Can I eat breakfast first?"

"All right! But hurry up. And put your dishes in the sink. Nellie and I are going now."

The girls picked for two hours. As they carried a washtub of flowers between them, Marie said, "My back feels like it's going to break in two!"

"Mine too!" Nellie groaned when they set down the tub and went back for the second one.

Dr. Withrow acted pleased when he came out to get the flowers. "Two washtubs! That's a lot of flowers for two little girls to pick. Mrs. Withrow is going to be surprised." He gave Marie and Nellie each a dollar. "You girls worked hard. Now Agatha has her work cut out for her! I used to ride my horse in the parade, but now we're too busy getting the car decorated."

Thrilled at receiving so much money, Marie and Nellie enthusiastically thanked the doctor before running to change into the new dresses Ma had made for them. They'd waited impatiently to wear the new red, white, and blue dresses since the day Ma finished them. When Ma brought home the flag material, Pa was really pleased. "My two girls will look like real Americans!"

As her family piled into Pa's new Model T Ford, Marie felt a shiver of pride at the shiny, black car. Pa had worried about taking out a loan for $850 to pay for the car, but Ma convinced him to do it. Paddy climbed in front to sit between Ma and Pa.

Pa was barely out of the driveway when he stopped the car by Mr. Thompsen, who was walking on the road with his daughter, Lorraine, and son, Roy. "Want a ride to town?" Pa asked.

Mr. Thompsen hesitated a minute before nodding, "Sure."

Ma got out of the car to climb in back and Mr. Thompsen sat down in the front seat with Lorraine in his lap. Lorraine's brother sat in the middle between Pa and Mr. Thompsen. Speeding up again, Pa hit a big rut in the road. Although everybody was squeezed together tightly, their bodies bounced like rag dolls. Marie's head hit the roof of the car.

Rubbing her head and feeling dazed, she saw Mr. Thompsen open his door and lift Lorraine out of the car, putting her down in the grass beside the road. Ma opened her door and they all scrambled out. Lorraine lay sprawled on the ground, her head bleeding.

"What happened?" Ma cried.

"She flew forward and hit the windshield with her head. You walk home. I'll take her to the hospital," Pa said.

"No hospital. She's OK." Waving his arms and chanting strange words in his native Indian language, Mr. Thompsen danced around Lorraine performing his ritual until his daughter opened her eyes. Marie took a big breath; her mother made the sign of the cross and said, "Thanks be to God."

Ma dabbed at Lorraine's cut head with her clean white handkerchief. Helping Lorraine sit up she asked, "Are you dizzy, Lorraine?"

"No."

Ma and Pa helped Lorraine to her feet and into the back seat of the car. Ma's arm was around her and Marie sat on the other side, holding her hand. Pa and Mr. Thompsen pushed the Model T out of the chuckhole and they were on their way. As Pa pulled onto Second Street, they heard the boom boom boom boom of drums.

"We're in time for the parade!" Paddy shouted. After Pa parked the car, they rushed to Third Street. The street corner by Rauscher's was crowded with people and they jostled their way through, saying hello or waving to friends. As they finally got situated on the edge of the wood sidewalk, Pa said, "Looks like they brought in a good load of rocks to put down on the muddy street. This street was such a quagmire yesterday; McDonald's Dray Line was stuck and they had to get Lynch to pull them out with his dray line."

A flag bearer led the International Falls band, their shiny brass trumpets and trombones glinting in the sunlight. The drummers twirled their sticks as they beat their drums and Nellie said, "Oh, I love the sound of drums. They give me goose bumps." Marie and

Nellie waved to friends on the school float, a big hay wagon pulled by four horses and a sign that said, "You are welcome in our school."

The fire truck carrying men dressed to fight a fire went by with its siren blaring and bystanders put their hands over their ears at the racket. The noise didn't seem to bother the horse plodding along behind. Pa said, "It must be some politician campaigning for good roads." The horse carried one sign that read, "Muskeg Special," and another that said "Vote for good roads."

A group of women dressed in white like nurses, their blue capes flapping open and the American flags they carried blowing in the wind. "The Red Cross volunteers," Ma said. "Those ladies help a lot of needy people."

"Indians!" Paddy darted into the street to see them. The women wore beautiful dresses decorated with intricate beadwork and the men's shirts were decorated. Some of the men wore feather headdresses. "Can we go to the pow wow and watch them dance after the parade?" he asked.

"We'll see," Pa said.

"Here comes Mrs. Withrow!" Marie said. "Look, she's got her whole car covered with our flowers."

As the square-shaped black Ford went by, Mrs. Withrow caught sight of them and waved. Leaning her head out the window, she yelled, "Thanks for all the flowers!" Marie and Nellie grinned with pride. Nellie said, "Oh, her car looks so nice!"

Pa said, "You girls sure picked a lot of flowers. You can hardly tell there's a car underneath them."

Paddy said, "Hey! You didn't pay me for helping you this morning."

Marie and Nellie looked at each other, wondering how much they could get by with. Pa had heard Paddy and said, "Marie and Nellie worked hard all morning. You didn't help that much. Just give him a nickel from each of you."

An open-top Ford followed Mrs. Withrow's car. Three dapper-looking men wearing straw hats, two of the men in the roomy back seat, advertised "Hasselbarth and Somers, the men's clothing store." Ma said, "Their car doesn't have as many flowers as Agatha's. I'm sure she's pleased with all the flowers you picked for her."

When the parade was over they headed for the restaurant. "Hurry up!" Paddy was hungry and getting impatient because Ma and Pa stopped to talk to so many people after the parade. Ma proudly accepted compliments for the patriotic dresses she'd sewn for her daughters. By the time they finally reached King Joy Café, Marie's stomach was growling. Pa always insisted on going to the King Joy because he peddled milk and cream there and liked Pete Baumchen, the chef. Pete came out to talk to Pa before going back into the kitchen to cook an excellent dinner for them. When they finished eating, Pa teased, "Does anybody want to go to the moving pictures?"

Paddy jumped up, "Me!"

As they walked past Reuter's Grocery Store on the way to the Grand Theater, Marie peeked through the window. "See how spotless Mr. Reuter keeps it?" Marie often went with Pa to deliver milk and eggs. "Mr. Reuter's white butcher's apron is never bloodstained, either."

The Rauscher brothers across the street weren't as fussy. Their store smelled of cigars. Both Rauschers were nice, but Mr. Nick chatted with her more than Mr. Joe and often let her choose a piece of penny candy from one of the big jars filled with delicious treats.

Riding home from the movie, they talked about Charlie Chaplin's silly antics. While watching the funny little man, they had laughed so hard they could barely read the dialogue that flashed on the screen.

Then Pa got serious, as he always did on Independence Day. "We are lucky to live in America. We have so much more freedom here. During the Great War we didn't have to worry about soldiers over here fighting on our land and worry about getting shot. Times are good since the Armistice was signed in 1918.

"I don't ever regret leaving Ireland to come to America. We don't have the English King taking away our lands like the Irish do. We can vote for the mayor of our city, the governor of our state, and the president of our country. I want you kids to always be proud of your country and to vote whenever there's an election."

Paddy said, "We can't vote. We're not old enough."

Ma scolded, "Pa knows that. When you're old enough, he wants you to vote and be good American citizens."

"'Tis a better life here than anywhere else in the world. Always appreciate the beauty of life and be proud of our country. Sing the **Star Spangled Banner** for me." Marie started Pa's favorite song, with Nellie and Paddy chiming in. Pa sang lustily, "land of the free and the home of the brave!"

Next, they sang **America** until they got home.

Marie silently thanked God that she was growing up in the United States and not Germany or Ireland. She added, "And thank you for not letting my parents send me to reform school."

Chapter 37

THE GOLF PRO
August 1926

Ferociously hacking with the hoe, Marie attacked the stubborn weeds with deep roots. She liked the garden to look neat. The sky looked ominous with rainclouds and she wanted to have the weeding done before the rain began and muddied the rows.

Snapping a few peas from the vines, she stretched, holding her hand on her aching back. A car was parked at the side of the road and she wondered who was sitting there.

The car door slammed and a man walked over to the garden. Thinking it might be somebody lost and needing directions, Marie picked her way across the rows of vegetables.

"Hi. I watched you chopping with that hoe. You have a wicked swing."

"I'm trying to get done before the rain."

"I'm Ralph Buckman, the new gold pro at the golf course. I see you out here quite often on my way to work."

"I'm Marie Donahue."

"Do you golf?"

"No. We're too busy on the farm."

"If you ever have time, c'mon over to the golf course. I'll show you around."

"Maybe."

"Well, I'd better get to work. 'Bye."

"'Bye." Marie watched him walk away. Before ducking down into his car, he waved again.

If Ma had come out to the garden she would have been shocked to see Marie hoeing with a grin on her face.

For several days Marie kept the garden cleared of weeds and had the vegetables picked as quickly as they grew. She didn't tell her mother that she was keeping a sharp eye out for Ralph Buckman's car. The few times she spotted the car, she was too far away from the road to wave him down. Finally, she timed it right and Ralph stopped when he saw her a few rows away from the road. "Hi Marie!"

"Hi!"

"The garden's looking good."

"Thanks. Would you like some peas? They're coming good now."

"Sure. Mmm, these are good."

"I love peas out in the garden. When I shuck them for a meal, my fingernails and thumb get all green."

"Say, we don't have many people signed up to golf this morning. Do you want to come over and go for a walk with me on the fairways?"

"I'll check with my mother. If I can, I'll walk over."

"I'll look for you." Ralph gave a wave and got back into his car. Marie waited until he pulled away before running to the house.

"Ma, could I go over to the golf course for a little while? The golf pro asked me to come over to go for a walk."

"Golf pro! What golf pro? How did you meet him?"

"His name is Ralph Buckman. He stopped a week ago and talked to me while I was out hoeing. He stopped just now and said he'd show me the golf course."

"Sure, and that's why you've been working hard out there. You can go for an hour." She warned, "If you're not back in an hour, I'll send your Pa after you."

Marie raced into her bedroom to change clothes. Skipping more than walking, she covered the quarter mile to the golf course in no time. As she got closer, a feeling of shyness slowed her down until she saw Ralph running toward her. "He must have been watching for me," she thought. She forgot her fear and ran to meet him.

Ralph said, "Glad you came! C'mon, I'll show you around the course. We'll start at number one and work our way around."

"How many holes are there?"

"Nine. I can't believe you've never been here before when you live so close."

"Well, I've walked over here now and then when nobody was around, but I don't understand the game. We've never had time to play golf."

"Yeah, I can see that. You put a lot of time into that garden."

"I enjoy gardening, watching things grow. In the spring I ride the horse while Pa walks behind with the cultivator."

"What's a cultivator?"

"It digs up the ground, getting it ready for planting."

"Sounds too much like work to me."

"Where are you from?"

"Minneapolis."

"I went to Minneapolis last year. Nellie's heifer won a prize and our whole family went to the state fair. Minneapolis is awfully big."

"That's where my folks live. But now I'll go where I can get work. Maybe down south. I started golfing when I was young—my dad is a golfer and we lived close to a golf course. We didn't have a farm, so I grew up on the course."

Ralph explained the game of golf to her as they walked. When they finished walking the course, he offered her a soda.

"What time is it? Ma said I had to be back in an hour."

"Well, you have a few minutes. Sit here. I'll be right back. What kind would you like?"

"Strawberry."

Ralph disappeared into the old Fogarty house that had been serving as the country club since their farm was sold to the golf course. Marie sat on the grass and waited, enjoying this pleasant interlude from work. Ralph handed her a bottle of strawberry soda and asked, "Would you care to go to a movie tonight?"

Marie gulped her drink. "I'll have to ask my parents."

"I'll be leaving here at 5:00. Do you want to be over by the road and let me know?"

"Sure. Well, I'd better get back."

"'Bye. Let me know about the movie."

My first date! Speeding home before Pa came looking for her, Marie hoped they would let her go to a movie. She found Nellie and breathlessly told her about Ralph. "Do you think Ma will let me go? I'm scared to ask."

Nellie's excitement faded. "I don't know."

"Come with me." Nellie trailed Marie into the kitchen. "The golf pro asked me to go to the movie tonight. Can I go?"

Ma looked shocked. "Wait until your Pa gets home."

Marie crossed her fingers. Her parents were having a big discussion about whether she could go to the movie. Finally, Ma sighed. "Well, she's almost sixteen. I was only sixteen years old when you met me."

Pa said, "That was different. I was on my way to America. How long is this golf pro going to be around?"

Marie interrupted: "He said he'll be moving wherever there's work. He said maybe this fall he'd be going down south where they don't have snow and can golf all year long."

Pa said gruffly, "Get home right after the movie."

Marie's heart skipped a beat. "Nellie, what should I wear?"

She and Nellie checked the closet. Nothing looked good enough for a date with a golf pro from Minneapolis. Finally Nellie decided Marie had to wear her newest dress. Marie was close to the road picking vegetables when Ralph went by. "I can go!" she called when he stuck his head out the car window.

When Ralph drove up the driveway to pick her up she was waiting outside. Ma yelled out the open kitchen window, "Bring him in, Marie."

Marie told Ralph, "Ma wants to meet you. Pa, my sister Nellie, and brother Paddy are still in the barn doing chores" She introduced Ralph to her mother, who immediately embarrassed her when she asked Ralph questions about his family. He told her, "I grew up in

Minneapolis by the golf course. My father was a good golfer and he taught me how, then I worked as a caddy. I love the game."

Apparently satisfied, Annie said, "I'll bet you're homesick. Would you like to come for supper some night?"

Ralph acted pleased. "Tomorrow night I get off early. Is that OK?"

Marie enjoyed the movie and the popcorn, but was nervous about being with a boy from Minneapolis. In the car going home, she chattered about the banquet at the Nicollet Hotel and going to Dayton's.

When the car stopped in front of the house, Marie knew Nellie was peeking out the window because a corner of the curtain was lifted. Jumping out of the car, Marie said, "Don't forget about coming for supper tomorrow night."

Ralph said, "I'll come straight from the golf course."

"He's really good looking!" Nellie said as Marie walked in. "Do you like him?"

"I don't know. It's too soon to tell. He's coming for supper tomorrow night—Ma invited him."

Ralph complimented Annie on the meal over and over. He insisted he'd never eaten such a delicious meal. "My mother can't cook like this, Mrs. Donahue. It was so good, I couldn't stop eating. I'm stuffed!"

"Sure, and you just stop by anytime, Ralph. I like to see a person eat."

"Marie, you grow good vegetables. I never tasted such good potatoes before. Are your thumbs all green from shucking peas?"

"Yes!" Marie showed him the green stain on her thumb.

Ralph didn't stop by for several days, but Marie knew he was busy from the number of cars traveling down the road to the golf course. The men running Mando all seemed to like to golf.

"A watch! Look, Nellie!" Marie was speechless when she opened the gift from her parents on her sixteenth birthday. She couldn't believe her parents had given her an Elgin watch, one of the finest wristwatches made. Holding out her arm, she let Nellie admire it.

Nellie said, "Last year you got a ruby ring and this year a watch!"

Marie could only nod over the lump in her throat as she looked at her left hand decorated with the ruby ring and Elgin watch. She wondered how her parents could afford to be so generous.

Ralph had been coming for supper about once a week and Annie had invited Ralph to come that night. She did not tell him it was Marie's birthday and he acted embarrassed that he hadn't brought a gift. "I'm sorry I didn't bring you something," he said. While assuring him that she was just happy to have him there, she opened another surprise present. It was a china glass slipper from one of Pa's customers, Mrs. Casey. Whenever Marie accompanied Pa delivering milk, Mrs. Casey always stopped to chat.

Pa said, "Mrs. Casey asked where you were today. I told her it was your sixteenth birthday, and she made me wait while she wrapped it up." Marie picked Mrs. Casey a big bowl of raspberries the next day.

Marie went out with Ralph a couple more times, but when Ralph left at the end of golfing season, Marie felt no regrets. She was anxious to start high school.

Chapter 38

FALLS HIGH SCHOOL
1927-1928

Marie's junior year, school was delayed because the new high school was not completed. According to the paper, Falls High School would start two weeks late, but it was a month before construction was finished. The high school students had a lot of catching up to do after starting a month late, but it was thrilling to attend a grand new school. The most excitement was the indoor swimming pool.

"A swimming pool!" Nobody could pass the pool without taking a peek at it, exclaiming over a pool inside the school. Delighted at the opportunity to take swimming lessons, Marie learned quickly. She got an A in the class.

Basketball was fun too and the gym teacher asked her to join the basketball team. She couldn't believe it when Ma said yes and didn't complain about buying her the uniform: white sailor blouses and black satin bloomer pants. The girls all thought they looked very fashionable, but the boys hooted and jeered at the costumes. The day she made her first basket Percy McGauley was there. The next day at school he said, "I saw you playing basketball. Nice basket."

With a rush of excitement she shyly mumbled, "Thank you."

"As she turned to walk away, Percy called, "Hey! See you at the dance tonight?"

"Sure. I'll be there."

Energetic dancing defined the flapper era. Nellie and Marie were popular at the school dances because they had lots of stamina from farm work. Dancing the Charleston didn't faze them; they could outlast everyone on the dance floor. Marie still loved dancing the Highland Fling, but none of the boys knew it. Sometimes she and Nellie did it together.

The dances were held above the fire hall and the jailhouse. The boys enjoyed scaring the girls about the criminals held in the jail. But one night their teasing sounded more serious—there was a murderer jailed just below them. "What if he breaks out of jail and comes after you?" The boys grinned as the girls squealed with fright.

"Don't worry, I'll make sure nothing happens to you," Percy bravely assured Marie as he danced a waltz with her.

All the junior girls were buzzing about the Prom. There would be a banquet, then a formal dance, and they talked about their dresses incessantly. Ma had promised Marie that she could pick out material at Burton's to sew herself a new dress.

First, Marie had to decide whether to try out for the junior play. Miss Johnson, the English teacher in charge of the play, stopped Marie as she was leaving class to ask her to try out for the role of Sally. But between chores and homework, she was busy every night and wondered how she could fit in play practice. Deep down, she worried because she'd never done any acting. On the other hand, she liked Miss Johnson and it might be kind of fun.

On her way out of class on Friday, Miss Johnson stopped her. "Tryouts are on Monday. I hope you come."

After fretting about it all weekend, Marie made up her mind to audition if Ma gave her permission. Whispering about the play to Nellie while they did dishes, she didn't realize that Paddy was listening. He ran into the front room where Annie was sewing. "Marie wants to be in a play!"

"Paddy! I wanted to ask Ma myself!"

After hearing that Miss Johnson had asked Marie to audition, Annie gave her permission. "But remember, if you get the part you still have your work to do around here."

Concentration was impossible on Monday. She was so nervous and jittery, she barely heard the teachers. At least once in every class she changed her mind about trying out. Walking with Winnie Brown and Stella Roberson to English class, she said, "I'm not going to audition tonight."

They coaxed, "C'mon! We're going to. Winnie Lund and Joe Formick are both hoping to get a part. It'll be fun."

Winnie Lund stopped Marie in the hall after their last class. "Stella said you might not try out for the play. I'm so nervous I can hardly stand it but I'm still going to audition. C'mon! Walk over to the auditorium with Joe and me."

When it was Marie's turn to read, her hands shook. She held the pages with both hands. Miss Johnson was smiling at her from her seat in the audience and that gave her courage to say the first lines. As she read, her legs began to tremble. Afterward, she asked Winnie, "Could you see my legs shaking?"

Winnie said, "No. How about mine? I could almost hear my knees knocking together!"

When Pa picked her up she told him, "I wish I hadn't tried out!"

"Why?"

"I know I didn't get a part. I was so nervous I could hardly read. The lines are supposed to be funny, but they didn't sound funny at all when I read them, not at all." She felt depressed.

The next day, Marie was afraid to look at the bulletin board where the parts were to be posted. She kept her distance, sure that she had not gotten a part. As she was going to her locker when school was over, Winnie waved from the bulletin board. As she slowly walked toward her, Winnie yelled, "Sally! Marie, you got the part of Sally!"

"I don't believe it!" Sure enough, there was her name with Sally beside it. Now that she had gotten the part, she worried on the way home about whether she could memorize all the lines. As she walked into the kitchen, Ma turned to look at her. "I see by the smile on your face that you got the part."

As she sat at the kitchen table trying to memorize her part, Marie told Nellie, "I'm so glad we have electric lights now!"

Nellie said, "Isn't it something to walk into a room and just pull a string and the light goes on? We don't have to light those kerosene lamps."

"I probably couldn't even study my part if we still had kerosene lamps, it would be so difficult to read my lines. These electric lights are much brighter."

Ma grumbled now and then about her coming home late from play practice, but Nellie did some of her chores. "Nellie, if you get a chance you'll have to try to be in a play. It really is fun and it's a nice way to make new friends."

The week before the play opened, Miss Johnson told them how each character needed to dress and that they had to find their own costumes. Marie's heart sank when Miss Johnson said Sally needed several dresses for costume changes. What could she do? She only had two dresses—one for school and one for church.

She wrestled with the problem all evening. Staring into her closet did nothing to make dresses materialize. At rehearsal the next day, she stumbled over her lines. Hanging back while everybody left, she told Miss. Johnson, "I have to drop out of the play."

Miss Johnson looked shocked. "Why? You're doing such a good job. What's wrong?"

"I don't have enough dresses for all the changes."

"Is that all? We're about the same size. You can use my dresses. I'll bring some for you, don't worry." The night of dress rehearsal, Miss Johnson brought several dresses for Marie to try on. "I wore these in college. They should fit you perfectly."

The stagehands set up Falls High gymnasium for dress rehearsal. Miss Johnson's dresses helped her enter into the role of Sally and she didn't miss a single line. People laughed in the right places and she left rehearsal feeling confident. She told Nellie, "I didn't know I'd like acting so much. I just hope I don't get scared tomorrow night."

"Are you nervous?" Winnie asked Marie.

"I have butterflies!"

The boys peeked around the curtain to peer at the audience. "Look at all the people!"

Marie poked her head through the slit of the curtain. Paddy was jumping in the aisle while Ma and Pa stood looking for seats. Mrs. Johnson instructed, "Take deep breaths before your entrance to calm down. You'll all do fine. Go break a leg!"

Everything went smoothly. The audience clapped hard between each scene, which gave the young actors confidence for the next scene. A few times, Marie had to pause until the audience stopped laughing at her lines.

After the last curtain call, Marie felt deflated. All that hard work and now it was over. Winnie said, "I wish we could do it again!"

"You were so good, Marie. I loved the play," Nellie raved on the way home but Paddy said, "I didn't like it. You weren't funny, either."

Pa said, "Paddy, Marie did a fine job. Everybody laughed when she gave those ridiculous answers. Sure, and they made me laugh. 'Twas a good play and you did a good job, Marie."

Marie went to bed satisfied. Before drifting off to sleep, a thought flashed through her mind and she sat up in bed. *Prom is only two weeks away! I was so involved with the play, I didn't think about it. I have to make my dress!*

There was a crisis on Saturday and they didn't get to town for material. Pa had butchered Nellie's prize heifer on Friday. Nellie was in hysterics most of the weekend. "How could you kill my Tillie after she won a prize!"

Pa explained, "She should have had a calf by now, but she hasn't. You know we butcher the ones that don't breed."

"But not my Tillie. None of the other cows are as pretty as her."

Ma said, "We don't raise cows so they can enter beauty contests."

"Sure, and I hated to do it. But we can't afford to feed a cow that doesn't give anything back. We all have to work on this farm, 4-H queen or not."

Pushing back her own feelings of remorse that she couldn't start on her Prom dress, Marie tried to comfort tearful Nellie. Finally, deciding nothing would stop the flow of tears, Marie cleaned the house thoroughly so she could whisk through housework and start sewing the next Saturday.

In the afternoon, Pa tried a new tactic. He told Nellie, "I'm making arrangements to have Tillie's hide made into a rug for you. Sure, and you'll have Tillie forever. We'll have it made with felt edges so it will last a long time. What colors do you want?" Nellie cried all the harder, but by suppertime she had adjusted to the idea. On Sunday, she talked of nothing else but the new rug; she'd decided it should be red and green.

All the other girls already had their dresses bought or made. Each day Marie became more anxious until Ma finally met her after school on Thursday. At Burton's, Marie fell in love with a bolt of pink georgette. "Oh, Ma, I love this one."

"That might be hard to sew with, Marie."

"It's an easy pattern. I'm using the same one I used for the last two dresses I made—the blue dress for Nellie and my green one. It should go good." Annie paid for the material.

Marie couldn't wait. As soon as they got home, Marie spread the material on the front room floor and laid the pattern pieces on it. Worried about cutting something wrong, she took a deep breath and said a prayer before grabbing the scissors. Her knees got sore while kneeling on the floor, but finally the job was done.

On Saturday, after carefully pinning pieces of the bodice together, she sat down at Ma's treadle sewing machine. The material was fragile and kept puckering. Ripping out seams, she tried again. Now there were holes in the material. Ripping and sewing, she finally lost patience. Throwing the mutilated material down, she stomped off to her bedroom in tears.

Annie sat down at the sewing machine. She lost her temper almost immediately. Getting up from the machine, she said, "Marie, I can't do a thing with that material. It's impossible to sew with! Well, we can't afford to buy more material. You'll have to wear the dress Uncle Jim sent at Christmas."

"I can't wear that! It's a winter dress," Marie wailed.

"Wear it or don't go to Prom."

Nellie said, "That dress looks beautiful on you, Marie. Nobody will notice that it's a Christmas dress.

"Oh, no! It has long sleeves, a black velvet skirt, and a red chiffon top. It looks like a Christmas dress."

"Nobody is going to notice what you're wearing. They'll be too busy worrying about how they look," Ma said.

. Marie wasn't convinced. "Nobody will ask me to dance."

Prom night, Pa drove Marie to the high school. Feeling self-conscious, Marie walked into the auditorium to find her friends. Rows of long tables for the banquet were spread across the big room. As Marie looked for Stella and Winnie, she saw that all the girls were wearing summery, sleeveless dresses. Feeling miserable, she plunked down beside Stella. "Look at this ugly Christmas dress I had to wear."

"Marie, your dress is pretty. You look nice and we're going to have fun!"

When the meal was over, she had lost some of her self-pity. Percy, sitting with a bunch of the boys, had mouthed, "Save me a dance."

Marie danced every dance in her Christmas dress. The dress was warm, but it didn't slow her down.

Chapter 39

ROMEO
Spring 1928

Nellie and Marie were in the kitchen cleaning onions, putting them in bunches to sell. Teary-eyed from the onions, Marie opened the door expecting Joe Bush, the manager of Riverdale Dairy whom Pa had hired to castrate pigs so the meat would be better. Surprised to see three men, she blushed when Joe said, "And this lovely lady is one of the beautiful daughters of the house." Marie quickly explained she was crying from cleaning onions.

"These two brothers work for me at Riverdale Dairy." Joe pointed to the shorter brother. "That's Ed Karsnia. The thin one is Romeo."

Marie especially noticed Romeo, the taller brother with the romantic name. Not as handsome as Ralph Buckman, but his thin face looked kind and he wore a big smile. Marie led them to the barn hoping Joe wouldn't tell her that he knew very well where it was located. She hung around watching until it became too obvious that she wasn't needed.

Nellie, squinting at her through tears, asked, "What took you so long? I'm nearly blind from these onions."

Ignoring her complaint, Marie said. "We'd better fix a big lunch because they'll be hungry when they finish with the pigs."

The men ate heartily, especially Romeo. Marie lost track of how many slices of bread he ate. Seeing her glance at him when he took another slice, he said, "I like bread. This is really good. Did you make it?"

Annie smiled. "I did. I bake bread nearly every day. You need a little meat on those bones. You'd better come back for supper some time."

The Karsnia brothers became regular visitors as they dated the Donahue sisters. Annie fed them good meals. At the end of August, Romeo said, "Ed and I are going back to Frazee tomorrow."

Frazee! That was over two hundred miles away, a long drive. Stunned, Marie felt like her heart stopped beating. She didn't know how to react, what to say. After all, they had been dating often and he'd even kissed her a few times. The first time, they were standing in the doorway saying good night when he shyly asked if he could kiss her. She had told him yes, but he'd given her only a quick kiss before saying, "Good night. I'd better get walking home. Have to be up at 3:00 to milk the cows in the morning.

Marie had rushed upstairs to wave to him from the window before telling Nellie, "Well, he finally kissed me. I was beginning to wonder if he was ever going to get around to it."

As this memory flashed through her mind, it made her angry that now he was leaving. She asked sharply, "Well, are you coming back?"

"I plan on it. Joe Bush said he'd hire me again when I come back. My dad wants us to go to North Dakota with him. We can make good money picking potatoes in the Red River Valley."

Marie's rigid body relaxed as her anger evaporated. She gave him a goodbye kiss, longer than any other kiss had been. She felt an ache of loneliness that didn't let up until Romeo returned two months later. Nellie wasn't upset that Ed didn't return with him.

With his brother staying in Frazee and not sharing rent, Romeo worried about expenses, but his first day back at work he met a man named Jimmy Phelan who wanted to share the cost of a room. Relieved, Romeo was in a good mood when he walked out to the

Donahue farm after work. "Jim Phelan said he'd room with me above Frank's Variety store and share the rent."

Now that he was back from Frazee and working at a regular job, Romeo began courting Marie. Sometimes he was waiting at noon when she came out of school and would take her to the Chicago Café or Boston Café for a hot pork sandwich. "Are you sure you can afford this? Each sandwich costs twenty-five cents—that's fifty cents every time we go for lunch."

Romeo usually ate at Mrs. Klow's boarding house on Second Street. "I can splurge once in a while." Romeo made fifty dollars a month, but he sent twenty dollars home to help his folks with their rent on a farm in Frazee. Marie knew he didn't have much money left for himself.

Ed Karsnia came back to the Falls to drive Romeo home for Christmas. Before leaving, the brothers brought Christmas gifts for the Donahue sisters. The girls exclaimed over the fancy mirror, brush and comb sets. Nellie's set was blue and Marie's green. Nellie was pleased with Ed's gift, but their romance was not progressing as intensely as Romeo and Marie's.

The day before Fourth of July Romeo and Marie walked down Main Street after eating lunch at Chicago Café. Romeo stopped in front of Sher's Jewelry Store. Shyly he said, "How about an early birthday present?"

Marie said, I don't turn eighteen until July 16th."

"I know, but I saw something in here that I like. Want to look at it?"

Marie hid her surprise. "Sure," she said as she walked toward the door.

Mr. Sher looked up as they walked in. "Well, you brought the pretty girl herself." He reached down into the counter and brought out a velvet tray with rings. "Here you are, Miss." Marie's heart thumped.

Romeo picked up a diamond ring.

179

Marie blushed as she realized he was buying her an engagement ring. The stone was too big and she said, "This looks expensive. How much is it?"

Mr. Sher said, "Most girls don't worry about the price! That one is fifty dollars."

"That's too expensive." Marie looked through the rings until she found one with a smaller diamond. "Here's a pretty one. How much is this?"

"Twenty-five dollars. It's a pretty little ring, but the diamond in the other one is bigger," Mr. Sher said.

"This is the one I want," Marie insisted.

Romeo said, "I've saved my money from working overtime. I've got enough money for a ring with a bigger diamond."

Romeo had changed jobs, leaving Riverdale Dairy to work for "Gyppo" Anderson. He worked much harder at the new job unloading logs from a train and stacking them on a conveyor belt that carried the logs into M&O, the paper mill, but he made more money because of overtime. After one hundred hours of unloading logs, he'd saved twenty-five dollars.

"I know how hard you've been working." Marie handed the ring Mr. Sher and said firmly, "This is the ring I want."

Mr. Sher shook his head. "Never in my life have I seen such a thrifty girl. You're a lucky man."

Marie's heart danced as she hurried home to share the good news with Nellie and her family. The ring on Marie's finger meant that she'd soon be leaving to get married, but blinking back tears, Nellie managed to say, "Oh, it's so beautiful!"

It was the best summer of Marie's entire life. Walking with Romeo around town on the Fourth, introducing him to everybody and showing off her ring, she was so happy she thought she would burst. She hardly remembered anything about the parade except that her heart seemed to keep beat with the drums. Of course, she couldn't ignore the airplane honoring Charles Lindbergh, the man who had made a non-stop solo transatlantic flight in May. Paddy had shouted, "Look at that!"

Everybody clapped and cheered as the replica of a plane passed by with its sign, "The Spirit of St. Louie, International Falls." Lindbergh's flight had made them all feel proud, especially since he was from Minnesota. Marie discovered that Romeo was almost as patriotic as Pa as he stealthily wiped a tear from his eye.

The St. Thomas Church annual picnic was always one of the most exciting events of the summer because it was usually the only time they went to the City Beach. Summertime was too busy on the farm to drive ten miles for a swim. This year the picnic not only fell on her birthday, but she had her engagement ring and fiancé to show off.

Marie and Nellie did the Saturday chores at home while Ma went to town to get ready for Sunday's picnic. St. Thomas provided money for the groceries and the ladies in the League got together in the church basement to prepare them. Parishioners always brought a potluck of salads and desserts, the women competing for rave reviews. The picnic was the church's biggest moneymaker and the women worked hard to make it a success.

The other big money-raiser was a bazaar that ran for five days. The Catholic women had a good reputation as cooks and even Protestants came to eat during the bazaar. Each woman was assigned at least one day to help, and as their daughters grew older, they were brought along to help. Marie always offered to do dishes because she enjoyed working the hot and cold water faucets. *It's so fun to just turn on the faucet instead of hauling the water and then heating it on the stove!*

It was a beautiful morning the day of the picnic and everybody flew around getting chores done. They would pick up Romeo on the way to 10:00 o'clock Mass, then drive right out to the picnic. Ma had offered to help transport the food. "I told the ladies I've got three strong men to carry that food out of the basement."

Paddy asked, "Pa, Romeo, and who else?"

Ma said, "You! The girls and I will help, too. Agnes Anderson said she'd bring her son, Irvin, along. He's younger than you."

They helped in the makeshift kitchen at the beach until Mrs. Fogarty shooed them out, telling them to go have a good time. "Your turn will be coming to do the work soon enough," Miss Stone said.

Ann Fraser added, "And it looks like it won't be long before you'll be one of the old married women."

"Yes, show us your ring," Nora Benedix said. "Your mother told us the exciting news!" Marie held out her hand and the ladies gathered around to look, exclaiming how pretty it was.

They found a good spot on the warm sand and spread out towels. Marie was glad she could swim now. She tried coaxing Nellie into the water, but she wouldn't budge off her towel. Nellie was so afraid of water, she wouldn't even get into the indoor pool at Falls High School. Marie said, "Nellie, the water is really shallow here. Come out and wade." Nellie refused. Of course, Ma wouldn't let Paddy go into the water at all because the icy cold water might trigger another bout of Rheumatic Fever. He kept trying to sneak in, but Marie or Nellie would call him back out.

Marie waded into the water slowly but Romeo ran in and dived. She was barely past her ankles when he was back. "What's taking you so long?"

"The water's cold! I have to get used to it slowly."

"Does it ever warm up? Romeo asked.

"No. Rainy Lake never ever warms up because it's so big. Did you know it goes for miles and miles, way up into Canada?"

Although she couldn't swim as well as Romeo, they had a lot of fun playing in the water. Marie began shivering. Romeo said, "You'd better go in and warm up. Your lips are blue."

Marie splashed back to the beach and Nellie put a towel around her sister's shaking shoulders.

Romeo said, "I think I'll go dive off that diving board."

As she curled into the towel to warm up, she watched Romeo climb up the diving board ladder. People started pointing when they noticed him climbing up to the highest diving board. Sometimes swimmers climbed up there, but after looking at how far it was to the water, they climbed back down to the lower diving board. Few were brave enough to jump off it. Romeo executed a perfect dive, hitting the water headfirst with barely a splash.

Marie shaded her eyes to watch, waiting for his head to pop up. It didn't. Sounding worried, Nellie said, "Where did he go? I can't see him."

A man sitting nearby said, "That guy that jumped off the diving board hasn't come up yet." By now, most of the people on the beach were looking out at the lake where Romeo had disappeared. Marie stood up to see better. Still no Romeo. Nellie was beginning to cry and other bystanders were looking anxiously out at the lake.

Marie didn't know what to do. Fear clutched at her as she splashed into the water, not noticing the cold. She was up to her waist when she heard Nellie yelling. Turning, she looked in the direction that Nellie was pointing and saw Romeo strolling nonchalantly through the sand on the far side of the beach, smiling and talking to people.

She sloshed out of the water as fast as possible and grabbed her towel just as Romeo stopped in front of her. "Where did you go?" she asked angrily. "We were all worried!"

"What? I just swam over there."

"Nobody saw you come up!"

"I swam underwater."

Marie was shaking more from worry than from the cold water. She stomped off to the women's dressing room to get dressed. Stella Roberson came in. "Marie, Romeo sure is a good swimmer! Everybody's impressed!"

"Well, I'm not. I was worried sick."

When they sat down at a picnic table to eat, Annie bawled Romeo out. She took time out from working in the makeshift kitchen long enough to eat with her family. "I heard about how you scared everybody. People were shouting that somebody had drowned and Nellie came running to me in tears. When she said it was you, I nearly fainted dead away."

Romeo explained that he'd learned to swim on the river when he was a young boy. "In Frazee, the loggers piled logs onto the frozen river to store them for the sawmill. In the summer they floated on top of the water. I could swim under the logs for a long distance before coming up for air."

Marie asked, "Didn't your folks worry about you?"

Romeo flashed a mischievous grin. "My folks didn't know I could swim. The river was off-limits. My Pa worked in a sawmill and he would rage about kids swimming in the river. Pa thought kids and logs were a dangerous combination, so I sneaked over to the river."

Ma said, "Well, I guess so!" She sighed. "Now that I sat down, I can hardly get up again."

"Do you want me to help?" Marie asked her mother as she was leaving the picnic table. "No, you keep Romeo company," her mother answered. Marie felt a warm flush at her mother's kindness and thought, "She must really like Romeo!" After their long day in the fresh air, they were all exhausted and it was a quiet ride home.

The County Fair on the last weekend of July was the other highlight of the summer. Stella Roberson and Joe Kalar double-dated with Romeo and Marie on Saturday afternoon. It was hot and dusty as they strolled around the carnival set up downtown just a block away from Rauscher's. Romeo and Joe paid ten cents a throw trying to win a teddy bear or doll for their dates. Marie and Stella laughed as they watched them trying to outdo each other, but both kept missing. Plunk! Romeo turned around with a grin when the dart hit the target. Marie was thrilled when Romeo handed her the teddy bear he'd won. She'd always thought it so romantic when she saw a girl walking around the fairgrounds carrying something her boyfriend had won for her.

They acted as silly as little kids on the merry-go-round, riding up and down on the stationery ponies to the music from the calliope. When they got off, Stella said, "Now let's go on the Ferris wheel."

Marie, remembering Paddy scaring her at the state fair, was reluctant to ride on it again and tried to find excuses. "It's pretty expensive. Look, it costs twenty-five cents; the merry-go-round is only ten cents, we could ride it again a couple more times."

Joe marched up to the ticket window and Romeo followed. As the Ferris wheel worker buckled them in, Marie blurted out, "Now don't shake this car. I get too frightened." Stella giggled.

The champion teddy-bear winner became sick on the Ferris wheel. They'd only gone around twice when Romeo said, "I'm sick. I need to get off." Romeo was holding his mouth. As they swept past the attendant, Joe yelled, "Stop! This guy is sick!"

Romeo had to endure one more round before the Ferris wheel came to a complete halt at the ground. The second the attendant released the bar holding them in, Romeo dashed away. He came back white-faced and Marie insisted they should go home. Romeo apologized for not being able to stay longer, but Marie didn't care. "It was long enough," she said.

Chapter 40

WEDDING PREPARATIONS

1929

One hot August afternoon, Ma surprised Marie when she suggested that she shouldn't finish high school. They were in the kitchen canning beans from the garden. "I see no reason for you to go back to school in the fall."

"But Ma, I only have three credits left to graduate," Marie protested. "And I'm an honor student." The canning kettle filled with quart jars of beans was boiling on the stove, heating up the kitchen. Between the heat and Annie's words, Marie felt faint.

"There's so much work to do around here, I can't keep up. Sure, and we'll have a wedding to plan besides. You don't need a diploma to raise babies." Marie hated dropping out of school but Ma continued her badgering and ignored all her pleas.

Marie did not go back to school in September.

Matt offered Romeo a job. "I really need some help around here. I know what a hard worker you are and I've had too many drifters who don't earn their pay. I'll pay you as much as you were making at Riverdale Dairy." Although Romeo made more at his job with "Gyppo" Anderson because of overtime, he agreed.

Romeo worked for Matt for fifty dollars a month and Marie worked for her mother—without pay. The wedding date had to be planned according to the farm schedule. Summer was too busy for Pa, and Ma didn't want it at Christmas because that was too busy for her. Finally, her parents decided they could be married in October.

Marie and Romeo visited Father O'Dwyer at St. Thomas Church to make wedding plans. Father O'Dwyer said the bans had to be published three Sundays in succession to announce the impending marriage. Nobody could be married without the bans that included the statement: "If anybody has an objection to this marriage, it is your obligation to say it." Marie knew nobody would object.

The second Sunday after the bans were announced, Father Desrochers came out to the farm for a visit. He said, "I'll be the priest at your wedding. Father O'Dwyer has cancer and won't be able to do it. Are you still planning to be married? We've had another couple cancel their wedding."

Marie and her mother assured the priest that there had not been any change in plans. "As a matter of fact, Father, we picked up the dress today. Mrs. Brown made it and it turned out lovely."

As soon as Father Desrochers left, Marie pranced into the bedroom. Nellie followed behind and Marie handed her a blue cloche. "Look at this hat we found for you at Burton's."

Nellie said, "Do you think it's the right color? I can't remember what the material looked like."

"It matches perfectly. Mrs. Brown was working on your dress when we picked up mine and Ma took a scrap of material with her. When we went to Burton's to get my shoes and stockings, we found a white cloche for me and that blue one for you." Nellie exclaimed over the hat and tried it on while Marie undressed.

Shivering with excitement, she slipped on the cream-colored pongee wedding dress. Nellie held the white wool coat and when Marie put it on, Nellie draped a white fur shawl around her neck.

Nellie exclaimed, "You look like a movie star!" Circling Marie's neck, the fox's head hung down almost to her waist and the mouth opened to clip onto the tail. A white cloche hat completed the wedding finery and Marie modeled the ensemble for Nellie and Ma. With her white shoes and stockings and the new cloche hat, her outfit was perfect!

Cousin Kathleen had sent the fur fox shawl from Pennsylvania. The Doran family had moved to Scranton because Uncle Tom couldn't find work in International Falls. Pa said, "I've been to Scranton. It's in northeastern Pennsylvania, not far from Tower City where I worked in the coal mine. It was a big city back then and already soot-begrimed from all the factories. Lackawanna Iron and Steel Company was the biggest plant in Scranton at that time."

Minnie and her family had apparently endured some tough times after leaving the Falls, but now Uncle Tom and his sons-in-law had good jobs in a factory doing the same type of work they'd done in Scotland. Two years ago, Annie had enclosed five dollars in a Christmas card to Minnie. Minnie wrote back: "Without that five dollars there would not have been a Christmas for the Doran family. Sure, and it was a godsend. We're in South Scranton where lots of other Irish live. They've been kind to us, but everybody's poor and it's been real hard."

Annie went on a rampage after reading that letter. "Why did they move? Minnie was doing well here, making enough money to support them both." Minnie had worked as a nurse in Ireland and after they settled in International Falls, she established a maternity hospital in her home. Pregnant women came to stay at her hospital a few days before the expected due date and didn't leave until ten days after the delivery. Minnie charged twenty-five dollars for the care of mother and baby. When she had no patients, Minnie sometimes walked out to the farm to help Annie clean. Occasionally, Irish tempers flared when Minnie discarded items that her sister thought were still useful. On those occasions, Minnie walked right out and back to town, hardly pausing for rest.

Annie apparently had forgotten those occasions. She continued to protest that the move had been unnecessary. "Faith, and it was such good luck having my sister live here. She might as well still be in Ireland, I miss her so much."

Chapter 41

THE WEDDING
October 16, 1929

The wedding took place at St. Thomas Church on a Wednesday morning. Pa had grumbled about the church law that did not allow weddings on Saturdays. "Sure, and it makes no difference to the church that I have a farm to run."

Marie helped Annie with preparations for the wedding breakfast before hurrying to dress in her wedding finery for the 8:15 a.m. ceremony. Nellie, already wearing her blue bridesmaid dress, helped Marie slip the dress over her head. "Oh, Marie, you look beautiful," Nellie sighed. Happy for her sister, but knowing that their relationship would never be the same, she couldn't stop sniffing and dabbing at her red-rimmed eyes.

From the back of the church, Marie saw Romeo's friend, Jimmy Phelan, standing in front of the altar with Romeo. Her heart skipped a beat as she thought how handsome her husband-to-be looked in his blue suit with a pink rose boutonniere stuck in the lapel. Suddenly she felt so nervous, her hands shook, but the music started and Pa turned to her with a smile. "'Tis time to go."

Walking slowly down the aisle toward her husband-to-be, past the pews filled with neighbors and friends, she caught quick glimpses of people she knew: Jenny Baker with her brother, Benny;

Alice Gendron with her parents. Margaret Withrow waved at Marie as she passed the pew with her family. The Kane and Drummond families were there, and Judge McPartlin with his wife.

Marie could feel Romeo trembling as they stood in front of Father Desrochers. His hands shook when he put the wedding ring on her finger. The newlyweds rushed away without shaking hands in a reception line; they had work to do. Hurrying home, they put the coffee pot on and started breakfast. By the time the guests arrived for the wedding breakfast, the bridal couple had coffee perking and Annie's fresh bread and cinnamon rolls on the table.

Annie hurried into the kitchen. Putting on a new apron, she soon had bacon sizzling in black cast iron frying pans. When the bacon was done, she put it on a plate in the warming oven and used the grease to cook scrambled eggs.

By the time the last of the guests left, Nellie had almost finished washing the dishes. In a few hours, guests would return to the Donahue farm for a wedding supper.

The chickens had been killed and cleaned yesterday. Now, Annie began the process of frying them and preparing the rest of the meal. Potatoes and carrots, which Matt had dug from the garden a few days ago, needed to be peeled and squash put into the oven to bake.

Marie offered to help, but for the first time that she could remember, her mother shooed her out of the kitchen. She and Romeo went for a leisurely walk down the lane.

"Ma said Mr. Baker might play his flute when he comes out for supper. I remember one time the Bakers brought a man who was visiting from Scotland. He walked around outside playing the bagpipes."

Romeo said, "I've never heard the bagpipes."

"I didn't like them, but I like hearing Mr. Baker play his flute."

Annie set up a table in the front room with her best Irish linen, china, and crystal. Marie told her mother, "The front room might not be quite as fancy as the Nicollet Hotel, but the table sure looks elegant."

The bridal couple spent the night in the downstairs bedroom in the old log part of the house. It would be their bedroom until they moved to their small house just down the road. Marie felt a sense of satisfaction that, because she had chosen a less expensive wedding ring, Romeo could afford to pay ten dollars a month on their own house in Goldville. When Hadler-Linsten listed the house for $1,500.00, Matt had convinced his future son-in-law that it would be a good investment. Living with her parents would allow Romeo to continue making house payments. The house was rented out now but the occupants, who worked at the golf course, were so poor that they'd paid only one month's rent of ten dollars. The renters were so grateful when Marie brought them sausages to eat, she didn't have the heart to ask them to pay any rent.

In the morning Nellie came downstairs red-eyed and snuffling. Knowing how difficult it would be to get through her first night of sleeping without Marie, Nellie had invited Alice Gendron sleep with her. Alice complained that she didn't get much sleep because Nellie cried most of the night.

Marie said impatiently, "Nellie, how could you be lonesome for me? I was sleeping downstairs in a bedroom without a door."

Matt had offered his Ford Model T car to the bridal couple so they could drive to Frazee to visit Romeo's parents and relatives. Marie hadn't met any other relative besides Ed, and Romeo's father said they couldn't afford to come to the wedding.

Without telling anybody, Paddy had installed a foot accelerator in the car, allowing the gas to be controlled on the floor instead of at the steering wheel. Regulating the gas by foot made long-distance driving easier. Paddy proudly announced the night before the wedding, "I installed a new accelerator in 'Tin Lizzie.' I'll drive you to Frazee."

Marie shouted, "You're not coming on my honeymoon!"

Indignant that he couldn't go along, Paddy removed the new gadget. Now, still pouting because he couldn't go with them, he declared, "You'll notice I took the foot accelerator out. I paid for it myself and you're not using it."

Marie was glad to wave good-bye to her family. With a sigh of relief, she turned onto the highway. Romeo refused to drive Pa's car, saying, "You can drive. I haven't had much driving experience."

Marie had learned to drive several years ago, impressing Romeo when they first met. "Did your dad teach you?"

"No, I learned to drive before Pa had a car. Art Hammel, our hired man, bought a new car and he let me drive around the Golf Course road. We never went further than the golf course, but I learned fast." She liked to clue Romeo in on everybody's family history and explained, "Art was a nice man. Pa hired him when Art's wife died and he brought his son Clayton here to live with his sister, Ann Irvin. Bob and Ann Irvin didn't have any children and, so they helped raise Clayton. They have a beautiful home with hardwood floors. They're Paddy's godparents."

As they left the farm, a scary thought clutched at her stomach. Looking at her new husband, she asked, "Do you think your family will like me?"

"You're my beautiful bride. They'll like you."

Chapter 42

THE HONEYMOON
1929

Dreaming about their future as Romeo dozed, Marie was suddenly jolted back to reality. At Pelland Junction on Highway 71, just ten miles from home, the narrow gravel road turned beside the railroad tracks. Thinking the road went over the tracks, she missed the turn and drove into the ditch. Bounced rudely awake, Romeo looked out the window in confusion. "What happened?"

Trembling, Marie sobbed, "I thought the road went over the tracks and I missed the turn."

"Are you hurt?" Romeo asked, concerned about his bride.

"I don't think so."

Shoving hard at the door, Romeo squeezed out and ran around the car to open Marie's door. Tenderly helping her out, he put his arms around her and hugged her, trying to comfort her.

Just then, a car stopped. The driver asked, "Are you hurt?"

"No. The wife is just shook up a bit."

The man's wife got out and the couple scrambled down the bank to stand beside the car. The man asked, "Think it will run?"

"I'll check it out."

The two men looked under the hood, conferring on the damage, while the woman tried to comfort Marie. Marie was in tears as she told the woman about the accident. "We just got married yesterday and we borrowed Pa's car for our honeymoon. We're on our way to Frazee to meet Romeo's folks. Now I've ruined the car and his folks are waiting for us."

Romeo slammed down the hood of the Ford and said, "The battery is cracked and all the water ran out. But we can run it to Littlefork and get it fixed at the garage there. Marie, get in the car and start it so we can push it out of the ditch."

Reluctantly, Marie slid behind the wheel. The men easily pushed the car out of the ditch. "I'll stay behind you, make sure you get there OK," the other driver said.

"I can't drive—I'm too nervous." Marie slid over to the passenger's side; Romeo got in the driver's side. "I know my folks will hear about our accident before we get back from our honeymoon! Pa paid lots of money for this car—what will he say?"

Romeo reassured his bride that everything would be all right as they drove to the garage in Littlefork. While Romeo helped the mechanic fix the car, Marie paced the sidewalk in front of the garage.

It was a long ride to Frazee after the accident. Romeo looked surprised when Marie began to giggle, erasing the frown creasing her brow. "Do you think Pa will believe that a leprechaun jumped into my path and that's why I went into the ditch?"

Her new husband said, "You don't have to worry about your Pa. He won't care what happened as long as you aren't hurt. Besides, the car was easily fixed."

"The last time I wanted to blame the leprechauns was when Pa's gold nugget was missing." Marie confessed the sordid story to her groom.

Romeo squeezed her hand. "Your Ma and Pa should have known you're too honest to lie or steal." Marie turned her head, looking out the side window so he wouldn't see her lips quiver at his kind words.

It was dark long before they reached the Karsnia farm. Apparently they'd been watching for them because they came crowding out when the car stopped in front of the house. "What happened? We've been so worried about you."

Romeo's worried relatives enveloped Marie in hugs. Although it was after 9:00, supper was waiting for them. Both sets of grandparents were there to greet them—John and Annie Karsnia and Mr. and Mrs. August Wilkowski. The Wilkowskis had stayed in touch with their grandchildren, Romeo and Mary Angela, although their daughter Josephine died from complications eight days after Mary Angela was born on March 6, 1906.

Romeo had told Marie about his mother dying when he was only a year old. With two babies to care for, Louie Karsnia was eager to find a wife. "Somebody told Pa about a family living in North Dakota with several girls. Pa wanted a good farm wife, so he hurried off to North Dakota to visit Mr. Kovanty and look his daughters over. When he got to the farm, the marriageable daughter—Julia—had just gone to town to look for work. A brother hitched up the horse and wagon and raced to town to bring her back."

Marie said, "It sounds like they were anxious to marry her off."

"Well, probably. They were poor. She must have been willing to see him because she came right back. When she came to the door, Louie decided she looked pretty good. They didn't waste any time, either. He and Julia were married a few days later in Minto, North Dakota on a cold November day. That was in 1906 and she's always been real good to me," Romeo said. "She took good care of Mary Angela too."

Now, Julia brought them into the house and bustled about the kitchen, getting them fed. The others had eaten and were in the middle of a card game. They finished up their game, talking Polish fast and furiously. Marie wondered whether they were talking about her.

When Romeo's grandparents left to go home to the neighboring town of Perham, Marie was glad to go to bed. She was weary from the long drive and the strain of meeting everyone. Upstairs, she shivered as she undressed and tried not to touch the icy floor. She told Romeo, "It's really cold up here. It's a good thing I have you to cuddle up to or I'd freeze to death."

Two days passed slowly. Although Romeo took her to visit relatives every afternoon, he was usually gone before she got up in the morning. The very first morning she woke up she felt confused about where she was. Remembering she was on her honeymoon, she hastily dressed to go find her groom. Julia said, "He's gone to work with Louie. Louie files the big saws at the Frazee Sawmill and when Romeo came down this morning he said he'd like to visit it. So Louie told him to come along."

The next morning Romeo went out to help an uncle on his farm and Marie began feeling pangs of homesickness. Lying in bed trying to keep warm in the morning, she asked herself, "How can I be homesick? I was so anxious to get away. I sure didn't think I'd miss everybody so much. I wish Romeo's family would speak English instead of Polish. The way they look at me, I don't think they like me. I know they're saying things about me. Louie keeps saying I'm too skinny."

Louie liked his whiskey in the evening, making Marie nervous. Her parents never drank and she hoped Romeo wouldn't drink. When they went to bed the second night she asked, "Can we go home tomorrow?"

"I promised we'd stay a few days. I was going over to help at Aunt Martha's farm tomorrow."

The next morning, the homesickness was worse. She was surprised at how much she missed Nellie. She'd never been separated from Nellie before. Suddenly she remembered the June afternoon when she and her sister sat on the riverbank and Nellie had begged Marie never to leave her. "I wish I hadn't left," she thought. "I wonder if Nellie is missing me as much as I'm missing her? I even miss Paddy—I should have let him drive us!"

The last day of the honeymoon dragged. She could hardly wait for morning so they could leave. She was up, packed, and ready to go before daylight.

Giving Marie a good-bye hug, Louie shook his head. "Well, Romeo, she's pretty but she feels like a sack of deer horns. Not much meat on her. She'll sure never make a farmer's wife."

Marie knew her father-in-law was wrong. She would be a wonderful farmer's wife.

And she was.

Epilogue

Matt had a reputation for raising good cattle. Martha Cole, a local author published in 1979 wrote in her book **Nakoda:** "A cow was bought from Matt Donahue, a genial little Irishman, who had a homestead west of town. In the spring, Mattie the cow had a calf and sometime later, John was to take her back to the Donahue farm to stay overnight. Her father explained to little Martha, 'If you want Mattie to have another calf she has to go and be with a bull for a while."

In a booklet written by Ira Hinckley, **"Way Back When, An Early History of International Falls."** he stated: "Farming was an infant industry in those days. Very little land was under the plow. Most people who held land planned to plot it and become millionaires. One farmer who stuck to the land without illusions was one of my earliest acquaintances, Matt Donahue. Matt had been a miner at Rainy Lake Village and Mine Center and had settled on a claim which he called Goldville. Matt made a success of life, but by precept, by the host of friends he had. He raised a family and none of them ever went to bed hungry. He made his way without asking of anyone. I prize an intimate friendship with him, extending through all the years I have lived here. Good old Matt went to his reward in March of this year (1938)."

MARIE DONAHUE KARSNIA

At the time of the first writing in 2001, Marie was nearly 90 years old and living in her own apartment in Hampton Court. She loved to cook, bake, play cards, and visit with her family. As much as she loved her family, she took delight in beating them at cards.

Love of life continued until her death. Strange as it may seem to others, she enjoyed a Celebration of Life while she was still with us. One day, while talking about funerals, she said, "I want you to prop me up at my funeral so I can watch. Her daughters and I surprised her with a Celebration of Life, while she was still alive, in August 2006 at an annual Karsnia Sisters Gathering. She loved it! We shared a poignant time of memories, laughter and tears.

Getting too quickly out of her chair when the oven timer dinged that her bread was done, she fell and shattered her arm. Unable to survive surgery, she made the decision to be transferred from St. Mary's Hospital ICU to Solvay Hospice House on Friday, January 25. With her hospital bed rolled up, she conducted one-on-ones with each of her family before dying on January 26, 2008. She is dearly missed.

Knowing that others in her apartment complex did not have a large family to visit them, Marie once commented: "Nobody was jealous of me when I was raising twelve children on the farm without plumbing or running water. But now I think people are jealous of my wonderful family."

When Marie was 86 years old, she was chosen to participate as one of four elders in International Falls to tell her history to school children. Larry Long, a traveling troubadour, recorded the stories of the four pioneers and worked with the school children to compose songs based on their lives.

Marie told Kathy Gjertson's class of third graders her story about her life. "One of my sons died at age 18 from a cerebral hemorrhage, but the other eleven children are all married. I have 50 grandchildren and just had my 52nd great-grandchild. I have a wonderful family and I think I'm a very lucky woman. I've had a lot of people to love, and a lot of people to love me."

Marie's pride and love for her family inspired the theme of the song that the troubadour and the school children composed for her. At the Community Celebration held in October 1997 before a large audience, the children energetically sang her song, ***To Have So Many Love Me.***

"*To Have So Many Love Me*"

(Chorus)
To have so many love me
To have so many want me
How could I be
Lonely
Tonight.

From Ireland we came
To America
To get some land
Build a home
Raise a family *(Chorus)*

Fried tomatoes in a frying pan
Cooked in butter
Homemade bread
Every day
So proud to be your mother *(Chorus)*

Pillow case, pants, and sheets
Made from grain sacks
Long underwear
Standing up
Frozen on the line *(Chorus)*

Keeping warm by the kitchen stove
When the cold north winds blow
Everybody needs love to pull them through
Fifty-six great grandchildren in my arms
From thirteen raised up on the farm
Plus fifty grandchildren, I love you. *(Chorus)*

Bibliography and Resources

Information retrieved by personal interviews with Marie was invaluable. Her daily recordings in *Grandma, Tell Me Your Memories*, given to her from Janet (Rasmussen) Anderson and her family brought her memories to life. One line in the book often developed into a chapter. Pat Donahue's *History of the Donahue Farm* and *Donahue Farm* were also helpful. I appreciate the generous support from those I interviewed; a big thank you to relatives who allowed me to use events of people mentioned in the book.

Abstract of Title, Lot 24 of the Plat of Sha Sha Point. Property of Leo and Phyllis Karsnia.

Archives with 4-H records at Minnesota Extension Office.

Archives, Koochiching County Historical Museum.

Article by Laurel Beager in The Daily Journal, Thursday, May 9, 1996.

Bridges, Hal. *Iron Millionaire, Life of Charlemagne Tower*. Copyright 1952, University of Pennsylvania Press.

Donahue, Pat and Ethel. *Donahue's Farm*. Edited & Published in 1989 by Ernest Witmer.

Donahue, Patrick. *History of the Donahue Farm*.

Drache, Hiram M. *Koochiching.* Copyright 1983 by Hiram M. Drache. Published by The Interstate Printers & Publishers, Inc. Danville, Illinois.

Hinckley, Ira W. *Rainy Lake Legends, Recollections of Pioneer Days in Koochiching County.*

Johnson, Arnold J. *Development of Forestry in Koochiching county Through 1965.*

Karsnia, Marie Donahue. *Grandma, Tell Me Your Memories.*

Nute, Grace Lee. *Rainy River Country.* Copyright 1950 by the Minnesota Historical Society, St. Paul, MN.

Oral Interviews with Marie Donahue Karsnia. Conducted by Phyllis Karsnia, 2000-2001.

Oral Interviews with Austin Finnerty conducted during trip to Ireland April 2001

Oral Interview with 4-H leader, Rosemund Kucera, Conducted by Phyllis Karsnia, 2001

Oral Interview with Christy Bubolz Earley, Extension Educator. Conducted by Phyllis Karsnia 2001.

Oral Interview with Millie Savard. Conducted by Phyllis Karsnia, 2001

Oral Interview with Olive LaVigne, Conducted by Phyllis Karsnia, February 15, 2001.

Oral Interviews with Peggy Karsnia Foyt and Rose Karsnia Rasmussen, Marie's daughters. Conducted by Phyllis Karsnia, 2000-2001.

Pennsylvania Writers' Project, *Pennsylvania.* Copyright 1940 by the University of Pennsylvania.

Perry, David E. *Gold Town to Ghost Town, Boom and Bust on Rainy Lake.* Copyright 1993 Rainy Lakes Interpretive Association.

St. Thomas Aquinas Parish History.